# BEAUTY AND THE HUNTER

## ERIN BEDFORD

*Cover Design by Moonstruck Cover Design and Photography*

# Also by Erin Bedford

**The Underground Series**
Chasing Rabbits
Chasing Cats
Chasing Princes
Chasing Shadows
Chasing Hearts
The Crimes of Alice
Hatter's Heart
Cheshire's Smile

**The Mary Wiles Chronicles**
Marked by Hell
Bound by Hell
Deceived by Hell
Tempted by Hell

**Starcrossed Dragons**
Riding Lightning
Grinding Frost
Swallowing Fire
Pounding Earth

**The Crimson Fold**
Until Midnight
Until Dawn
Until Sunset

**Curse of the Fairy Tales**
Rapunzel Untamed
Rapunzel Unveiled
Rapunzel Unchained

**Her Angels**
Heaven's Embrace
Heaven's A Beach

Heaven's Most Wanted

## House of Durand

Indebted to the Vampires
Wanted by the Vampires
Protected by the Vampires
Embrace of the Vampires
Tempted by the Butler
Loved by the Vampires
Huntress of the Vampires

## Academy of Witches

Witching On A Star
As You Witch
Witch You Were Here
Just Witch It
Summer Witchin'

## Children of the Fallen

Death In Her Eyes
Fire In Her Blood

## House of Van Helsing

Her Cross To Bear

## Fairy Tale Bad Boys

Beauty and the Hunter
Wendy's Pirate

The Beast of the Fae Court
Granting Her Wish
Vampire CEO

# Beauty and the Hunter

## ERIN BEDFORD

# CHAPTER 1
## *JASON*

IT'S THE QUIET ones you have to watch out for. The mousey kind of women with their nose buried in a book, day in day out, not paying any mind to the real world. The ones waiting for Prince Charming to sweep them off their feet. But in Jason's experience, those were the women who were the most fun.

The girls who would call him up in the middle of the night for a quick fuck in the backseat of his car. The ones who want him to choke them out while he was balls deep inside of them—kinky shit like that.

Isabel was that kind of girl.

It was one of the many reasons his eyes tracked her slender form as she made her way down the aisles. Her brown hair pulled up high in a ponytail so that with each step, it bounced just above the shelves. Jason's hands gripped the counter in front of him as he fought to restrain himself.

Patience, man. Patience. You don't want to scare her away.

Like with any good quarry, you had to know when to watch and wait. Some of the best catches were the ones who came to you. Then when they were right where you wanted them, that was when you went in for the kill.

A wicked smile curled up onto his face as he watched the ponytail lose its peppy bounce and became more of an aggravated jolt. His breath caught as the ponytail paused in the middle of the rifle cleaning supplies. After a moment, a frustrated growl came from the aisle, and it was like music to his ears.

He leaned forward on his elbows, anticipation curling in his stomach. He could just picture the anger that would fill Isabel's chestnut eyes when she realized he was working the counter. The scowl that would cover her face caused him to harden at the thought.

All those images did nothing to prepare him for the electricity that shot down his spine when those eyes finally landed on him. Her brows scrunched down and her eyes narrowed as she stomped up to the counter.

God, she was beautiful.

As she stopped in front of him, he put on his biggest megawatt smile that would have the girls back at the bar, creaming their panties. But not Isabel. She took one look at his smile and scowled harder.

"Hello, ma'am. What can I help you find today?" It was a rhetorical question. He knew exactly what she was there for thanks to the call from Earl down at the hardware store, telling him she was coming his way. Not that she knew that.

It was one of the benefits of living in a small town. Everyone knew everyone and their business. That meant they all knew about his and Isabel's falling out. It would have bugged him more if most of the town wasn't on his side. Which was why she was standing in front of him now looking for mouse traps at his outdoor and sporting goods store rather than Earl's, who had conveniently run out just as Isabel came in.

"Where's Peter? I thought he was working the Saturday shift?"

Ah, so she had checked to be sure he wasn't going to be there.

Peter usually did work the weekend shift, leaving him as the owner, to be off on the weekends. Not that he had much going on without Isabel waiting for him. It was lucky for him that he'd stopped by the store to grab his phone, or he'd have missed Earl's call and the delicious opportunity before him.

"He's on a break."

She pursed her lips at his response, and then growled out, "I need mouse traps." Her nose scrunched up, causing the cute freckles on her face to stand out more.

"Mousetraps, you say?" He stroked the strong line of his jaw, pretending to think about her request.

"Come on, Jason. Don't fuck with me." She stomped her sensible black flats, the effort wasted on the wood floors, barely making a sound. "I know you have them. Earl's out until their truck comes in next week."

"Then wait until next week." Jason purposely dragged out the conversation just to hear her curse again. The only other time he could get a less than perfectly articulated response from her was when he was pounding deep inside her. Then she was all dirty talk and curses that were creative enough to make a sailor blush.

"I can't, or I wouldn't be standing here right now." She placed her hand on her hips. "They've already eaten five of my spreadsheets. I had to start all over again, putting me way behind schedule. Now Earl said you were the only other place in town that would have them. So, I suggest you stop trying to vex me and hand them over."

"Now hold on a moment, Izzy. Just because I stock hunting traps doesn't mean that I have traps for everyday occurrences like a little bitty mouse." He pinched his fingers together, a smirk covering his face.

"Don't call me that!" She placed her hands on the counter, and his eyes were drawn down to her chest that was pressed against the edge of the bar, giving him a magnificent view of her cleavage. "Jason. Are you listening to me?" She snapped her fingers in front of his face, ripping his gaze from the delectable sight of her chest.

"Yes. Mousetraps." He pointed a beefy finger toward the back of the store. "Back wall, top-shelf."

She glanced over her shoulder to where he had pointed. Muttering thanks, she marched back down the aisle.

His eyes followed her curvy behind as her petite form thundered toward where he had moved the mouse traps just moments before. Jason inched around the counter and sauntered down after her. A smile filled his face as he watched her stand on her tiptoes, trying to get to the packages just out of her reach.

"Need a hand?"

His voice was right beside her ear, causing her to jump in place. She spun around and glared at him, her hands on her hips once more.

She was so hot when she was mad. Jason wanted to take her in his arms and cover her smart mouth with his. From the way her breath caught in her throat at his presence, he wasn't a hundred percent sure she would tell him no.

"Here." He reached over her being sure to press close as he pulled down a few traps. "Should I put them on your tab?"

Isabel took the traps from his hands, their fingers brushing, causing a zing to go through him. From the widening of her eyes, he knew she felt it too.

"Yeah, thanks." She tried to push passed him and beeline it for the door, but he caught her arm.

"Wait."

Isabel looked down at the hand holding onto her and then up at him.

"What is it? I really need to get going. I have a ton of errands to run before Vincent gets home."

The sound of the monster's name caused him to drop her arm like it was on fire.

Vampires, fairies, even werewolves were common occurrences in big cities. There were also a few senators who were part of the undead—an effort to bring equality to the supernaturals of the world. But, in Rollings, Minnesota, where the population didn't go higher than five thousand, the sups were a lot harder to come by. The ones they did have were well known, and Vincent was one of the most notorious of them all.

Vincent was a werewolf who owned the only gambling hall in Rollings. If being a supe wasn't bad enough, he lived in the gaudiest mansion just outside of town and was the son of the alpha who ran all the Minnesota werewolf packs. Making him some kind of royalty to the other supernaturals.

But not to Jason. The only thing he cared about was that the wolf was Isabel's boss, boyfriend, and the only thing standing between them getting back together.

"Right, Vincent," he drawled out, trying to hide his irritation. "How is the mutt doing?"

"He's fine," Isabel quickly replied, stepping back from him. "Look, I really have to go."

With that, she hurried out the store door, causing Jason to frown at her retreating form. She hadn't even acknowledged his insult on the mutt. It was not like her at all.

Throwing his work apron on the counter, he called out to the back room, "I'm heading out for a few, cover the front."

"You got it, boss." Peter, his teenage part-timer, came back to the front, instantly taking his phone out of his pocket and typing a mile a minute.

Shaking his head at the kids of this generation, Jason stepped out of his shop and onto the bustling crowd of Rollings citizens running their Saturday errands. At 6' 2" it wasn't hard for him to see over the group, but with Isabel barely reaching his chest, it was like finding a virgin in a Mardi Gras parade.

Eventually, his attention was drawn to the bell of what he knew was Isabel's favorite store in three counties. Spines and Dust. The only new and used bookstore in all of Rollings. Why she liked to buy her books in person rather than online was beyond him, but at that moment, he was thankful for her little quirk. He took off toward the store just as a bouncy ponytail disappeared inside.

# CHAPTER 2
## *ISABEL*

EVEN WITH HER back to the door, she knew the moment Jason stepped into the store. He had the kind of presence that was hard to ignore, and boy did he know it.

Built like a linebacker with his black hair and dark penetrating eyes, he was the very definition of tall, dark, and handsome. Not a woman, man, or child in Rollings was left unaffected when he went by. Isabel was no different, she was just better at hiding it.

Most of the time.

Trying her best to ignore the eyes boring into her back, Isabel shoved another book into her basket. She loved this store. It had all the newest works by her favorite authors, as well as the older ones. The ones that were aged to perfection, giving them each their own unique smell and character. She was one of the few patrons of Spines and Dust who actually appreciated the combination.

Jason sure as hell wouldn't be caught dead in there if she didn't drag him kicking and screaming the whole way. Which brought up the question of why he was there? The only reason she could think of for him being there was her.

Eyes down, she pretended to focus on the back of her book, and that she didn't notice his shadow looming over her. If she didn't acknowledge him, would he go away? The sound of his throat clearing said the chances of that happening were slim to none.

"What do you want now?" She retorted, not looking up from her book.

"Now, don't get your panties in a twist, Izzy. I just want to talk." The sound of his voice was deep and husky. It always made her think of naughty bedroom things. She shook her head at the thought. She was with Vincent now, and he was everything she wanted. Vincent was kind and generous. So, what if the sound of Jason's voice made her weak in the knees. He was a boorish pig. Didn't he prove that when they broke up?

"I told you to stop calling me that." Closing the book in her hand with a snap, she placed it in her basket before heading further into the store.

Saturday morning was the best time to browse at her leisure. Most of the younger crowd wasn't awake yet, and the adults were too busy trying to get their errands for the week done. Leaving the store practically deserted. Usually, she would crave the solitude but with Jason on her tail, it only made the air thick with tension.

"What would you have me call you?" Jason asked, his long legs keeping up with her attempts to lose him. "Belle?"

"No. Not that." She winced at his use of Vincent's nickname for her. Vincent was a wonderful boyfriend and an even better listener. The moment Jason had heard her name, he insisted on calling her Belle because she was more beautiful than any rose he had ever seen. His words, not hers. But the sound of it coming from Jason's mouth seemed wrong in more ways than one. The most glaring reason being the real reason she was sure he was there.

"What about sugar?" This time, his voice was low and hot in her ear. The only time he ever called her a pet name was when he was on the verge of coming. His use of it then in broad daylight caused her body to react the way it was conditioned to. Her face flushed, and a throbbing ache made her press her thighs together.

"Isabel." Her voice came out hoarse and a bit breathless. Stop it. He's not that hot. She chided herself for acting like a cat in heat. She cleared her throat and took a step back from him. "Just Isabel."

"All right, Isabel. Whatever you say." A knowing smirk crept up his face as he took a step closer to her, causing her to back up until the shelf bumped her back. Caged in by his massive arms, she focused on pinning him with a glare and not the rampant beating of her heart.

"Seriously. No more games, Jason. What do you want?" The words were meant to cool his heated gaze but had the opposite effect when his hand came up to brush a stray hair behind her ear.

"I just wanted to see how you were doing. You seemed kind of tense back at the shop." His dark eyes drilled into her daring her to deny it.

"Like I told you before, I have a lot of errands to run, and then I have to redo all those spreadsheets for this month's ledgers, and all before Vincent gets back from visiting the pack tomorrow." She brought up Vincent's name in an effort to remind herself who she had promised herself to. Not that it was helping any.

"He's been going to visit his family a lot lately, hasn't he?" Jason trailed a finger down her arm, causing goosebumps to rise in its wake. "Is that why you are here, buying dirty books, instead of working on those spreadsheets you are so worried about?"

Her face filled with warmth at his question. She had hoped he hadn't noticed what was in her basket. Though, it was hard not to when every single one of them had a shirtless man or a woman in mid-orgasm on the front.

"Tell me, Iz." He leaned in closer until their noses almost brushed. "Is the mutt taking care of you like you need to be? Does he know when you get stressed all you need is to come a few times, and you are right as rain? Like the one time I pulled over on the highway, do you remember that baby?" His fingertips tickled the tops of her thighs, and she fought her body's need to arch into his touch.

Isabel gulped. She remembered all right. She had been ranting and raving about her current client at the time, an eco-crazed hippy that didn't know that to be a successful accountant, she needed receipts. A purchase for a hundred dollars or so at someplace over in Saint Paul for something he didn't quite remember was not tax-deductible. So, after they had been going down the highway for a good fifteen minutes of her harping, Jason had pulled over and hopped out without a word.

"What are you doing?" She'd asked when he had opened her side of the door, only to cry out in surprise when he flipped her around, threw her skirt up, and buried his face between her thighs. She had never orgasmed so hard in her life.

"No. I don't. And Vincent does just fine," she forced out, pushing her basket between them so Jason would have to take a step back.

"I don't believe you." Laughter filled his voice at her attempt to push him away.

"Well, it's a good thing I don't care what you think." She sniffed. "Now if you would excuse me." Isabel shoved her basket further between them and marched back toward the front.

"Well, now that's a good thing." Jason clucked his tongue as he followed her.

"Because I know you and you only read that trash when you are frustrated. So, it can only mean that dear old Vincent isn't hitting all your buttons."

Damn him. Anger filled her at his words, mainly because he was right. Not that she'd tell him, but she and Vincent hadn't done more than kiss yet.

After she went to work for Vincent as a way to pay back her father's gambling debt, she found herself falling for the quiet and reserved werewolf. It wasn't an epic passionate love like in her books but it was comfortable. Unfortunately, after their one romantic moment where they declared their love for each other, Vincent had kept his distance.

The charming werewolf she had become endeared to was becoming little more than a stranger every day. Besides the daily peck on the lips when he left or came home from work, her sex life was pretty much nonexistent. After being with Jason, it was hard to go from mind shattering orgasms almost every night to nothing. It was enough to make any sane woman turn to erotica.

"Whether he is pushing my buttons or not is none of your business." Isabel spun on him, pointing a finger at his large muscular chest. "You cannot come in here and start acting like you have a say in my life, in case you have forgotten, you are not my boyfriend anymore. Vincent is. Now, if you are quite finished harassing me, I have other errands to attend to."

She turned on her heel, her basket clutched tight against her side, causing it to bite into her arm. When she reached the end of the aisle, she almost breathed a sigh of relief at his lack of response. She was about to step out of the aisle when she heard a half audible response.

"What?" She turned to look at him and regretted it the moment she saw the dark look in his eyes.

"Fiancé." His size thirteen boots stomped down the aisle. "The mutt may be your boyfriend, but do not try and compare what we had to something as fleeting as that. Don't forget, nine months ago, you were singing a very different tune."

"And whose fault is that?" Isabel hissed trying to keep her voice low, even though she knew Mr. Goodman, the sixty-year-old owner of Spines and Dust, was listening to every word.

Jason barked out laughing. "You can't tell me that brute makes you happy?"

"Brute? That's a bit funny coming from the likes of you." She crossed her arms over her chest. "At least Vincent respects me and my intelligence."

"Oh, we are going to bring that up again." He threw his hands up, exasperation clear on his face.

"Yes, we are. You seem to forget the very reason we broke up to begin with." She actually hated bringing it back up. The thought of the last time they had been together and the argument they had always caused a small sting in her heart. Nine months later, he was still continually apologizing and scheming to get her back. She was through playing nice.

"I'm not going to apologize anymore." He crossed his bulging arms over his chest. She remembered a time when she loved to be wrapped up in those arms, but that was before.

"Good, because I'm tired of hearing it." She stepped closer to him, her eyes challenging him.

"Fine." He leaned down until he loomed over her. "I hope your books and batteries keep you warm at night because you and I both know Vincent sure as hell won't."

He pushed passed her, his path directed toward the exit. Her eyes followed after him, and before she could stop herself, her eyes began to linger on the way his jeans fit his backside. Irritated that he still had such an effect on her, she yelled after him.

"They will!" Before snapping her mouth shut at what she had just agreed to.

Glaring at the smirk he tossed back at her, she marched up to the front counter where Mr. Goodman was failing miserably at pretending not to eavesdrop. She began unpacking her books and didn't turn from the counter until she heard the bell of the door sound his exit. Letting out an aggravated breath, she muttered under her breath about the bullheadedness of some men.

"Well, that didn't go very well, did it?" Mr. Goodman commented as he rang up her order.

Frowning at the older man's pity filled eyes, she murmured, "No, it really didn't."

# CHAPTER 3
## *JASON*

SLAMMING BACK THE shot, Jason grimaced as the burn of tequila slid down his throat and settled in this belly. He didn't do shots often, and when he did, it was usually for a good reason. Izzy was always a good reason.

As he gestured for the bartender to pour him another, a delicate hand slid across his shoulder, and a large chest pressed against his side. His cock twinged involuntarily, though he could care less about the tramp hanging on his arm.

"Hi, Jay." The voice tried its best to sound sultry but came out more of a rasp. Jason didn't need to turn his head to know who was by his side. The lack of a reflection in the mirror behind the bar answered that well enough.

"What do you want, Monica?"

"Don't be like that." She pressed her breasts more firmly against him, trying to draw his attention to them. "We could have some real fun, you and I."

Jason finally turned from his drink to look at the brunette. Blood red lipstick covered lips that pouted up at him and dark lined eyes leered up at him with lust and hunger. The latter emotion was probably the more dominant of the two.

"Even if I was on the market, you know I don't date sups, Monica."

His words didn't deter her. Monica used her vampiric strength to hop up on the bar and crossed her legs in front of her, giving him an excellent long glimpse of them underneath her barely legal short skirt.

God, he needed another drink.

"Not even for an old girlfriend?" She tiptoed her fingers up his bicep, leaning forward to tempt him with a look down her tight corset.

He and Monica had dated back in high school. Back before the supernaturals had come out of the closet, back when she had a heartbeat. She was actually one of the first ones to turn when given a chance at eternal life and beauty. Not that Jason was surprised. She was as vain then as she was now. Death hadn't changed that.

Jason pushed her hand away and frowned. "Not even then."

She huffed and dropped from the counter. "You know, Jason. I'd go animal for you if you'd give me half a chance."

He sighed and tossed back the shot the bartender had placed in front of him. He watched the mirror where he knew she was standing, though no reflection was found.

"It's pretty to think so, Mon. But you're a monster, it hurts but it's the truth. You can't help what you are, and I wouldn't want you to try to be anything less."

"Fine." Her fangs snapped together. "But when you're tired of running after Miss Nobody, you come and give me a call. I might answer."

The sound of her stilettos stomping across the floor trailed after her and all Jason could do was sigh. He should have gone home to get trashed. With it barely being after sunset, he thought he would be able to get in and out without a fuss. Still, his popularity seemed to have other ideas.

Placing his head in his hands, he thought about closing his tab out and going home when the door to the local bar, Caver's, slammed open. The distinct sound of his best friend, Luis, causing a ruckus as he made his way into the bar.

"Jason!" He exclaimed, clapping him on the shoulder. "It's good to see you out and about."

"Hey, Lu." Jason took a sip of the beer in front of him and nodded at the bartender to give him another shot. He would definitely need to be intoxicated for this lecture. He loved Luis like a brother, but he was a guy who only had one thing on his mind. Having fun and getting laid. Two things that had become less important to Jason since he'd met Izzy.

"You started the party without me, I see." Lu gestured at the four empty shot glasses in front of him. "That can't be good."

"Don't start, Lu." Jason shot a warning glance at his friend.

"Hey, I'm not starting anything." Lu held his hands up.

He and Luis had both joined the military straight out of high school and even at 5' 9" he was still just as muscled. While Jason had chosen the quiet life of a shop owner, Lu had become a deputy for the sheriff's department, claiming he needed more excitement in his life. Jason thought his friend was way too laid back for the kind of person a police officer would need to be. Too eager to choose the nonviolent way out.

Some called him a wimp, but Jason had learned the hard way that just because Luis was smaller didn't mean that he was weaker. He still had the scar on his jaw to prove it.

Jason slammed the other shot, his eyes beginning to blur. "I've had a shit day, and I don't need you to make me feel worse."

"You went to see her again, didn't you?" When Jason didn't answer, his lips twisted down in a frown. "Man, I've told you a thousand times. Why do you keep torturing yourself like this? She's with him now. The best thing you can do is move on, and if life brings you back together, then so be it. Are you going to waste your best years chasing after a woman who doesn't want you?"

Jason grabbed Lu by the scruff of his shirt. "You don't know what you are talking about."

"See, man, this girl has got you all kinds of messed up." He looked down at Jason's hands holding him not doing anything to get away. "Since she came to this town, all you think of is Isabel. It's about time you think more about you and what you want."

"But what I want is her." Jason let go of his friend's shirt. The threat was no longer meaningful.

Lu shrugged his shoulders. "Sometimes, to get what you want, you have to get what you need." His eyes flicked behind Jason's shoulder, and a broad smile filled his face. "And what I think you need is a nice night out with women who actually wants you."

Jason opened his mouth to protest, but Lu beat him to it.

"Now hear me out. You don't have to do anything you don't want to do. This is just hanging out with a couple of beautiful women who happen to adore you." He shrugged, trying to be nonchalant. "And if something would happen to happen, not that it has to, all the better."

Reluctant to admit he needed a distraction from all things Isabel, Jason growled and crossed his arms.

"Fine. Where are these women you speak of?"

Lu's grin widened, and he spun Jason around to point at the corner of the bar where two matching blonde heads bent close together. The bodies that went with those heads he knew belonged to twin sisters, who had matching blue eyes and wandering hands. He'd had to untangle himself a time or two from their clutches.

"The Trainer sisters?" He looked over his shoulder, raising an eyebrow at his friend. "Really?"

"It'll be fine." Lu gave him a little shove off his stool. "Nothing has to happen if you don't want it to. But at least you can relax in knowing they are a sure thing."

"Sure thing, my ass," Jason grumbled but let himself be steered over to the table where the blonde heads had popped up and began to giggle and flirt at his approach.

He should have just gone home.

# CHAPTER 4
## *ISABEL*

BY THE TIME she arrived home it was well after dark and her mood had not improved. The house was quiet, the staff had all but retired for the night. When Vincent was there, it would have still been bustling with life, but with it only being Isabel, things were a bit laxer.

Not that she minded, she actually preferred to be left to her own devices. Though, it was still a bit odd to be waited on hand and foot. Some nights, like tonight, were nice not to have to worry about finding her own dinner.

Making her way to the kitchen, she peeked into the fridge to see what was available. There were multiple containers full of leftover food from previous days: lasagna, pasta, meat, and potatoes. If there was one thing the chef was good at, it was making more than enough food to go around and fattening enough that Isabel had to be careful how much she ate, or she would blow up like a balloon.

Grabbing a container of last night's dinner, she popped it in the microwave and browsed through her selection of books she carted in. Reading over the back of several different ones, she was beginning to see a particular trend. Every book featured a hero who was arrogant, dark-haired, and a bad boy.

Throwing her books down, annoyed at how obvious she was, she grabbed her food out of the microwave. Then fished out a fork out of the drawer and decided at the last minute to tuck one of those books under her arm.

So, what if she had a thing for bad boys. It was just fiction. Not like she was acting on it.

Vincent was in no way a bad boy. Sure, he ran a casino, and Vincent was a werewolf, but that didn't make him a bad guy, just different. He was considerate and kind, two things that did not scream her typical type.

When she arrived at her room, she sat her meal and book down as she proceeded to change into her pajamas. It was barely eight o'clock, but if she was going to get down and dirty with a backwoods cowboy, she wanted to be comfortable doing it.

Thirty minutes and a stomach full later, she was already getting hot and bothered by the intensity of her book. The main heroine, Jill, was a mousy librarian who turned out to be a closet submissive. That was until she met the irresistible, Henry, who wanted to give Jill as many orgasms as possible. Written to get the fire burning, it was doing a good job giving Isabel's already strained self-control a workout.

Fingers itching to relieve the tension between her legs, Isabel set the book down. She headed to the bathroom to take a nice long and hopefully orgasmic bath. Though, before Isabel could get two feet from her bed, her phone buzzed. She hesitated and almost ignored it before thinking it could be Vincent.

Grabbing her phone, she flipped her finger across the screen to see not a phone call but a text message. From Jason. Biting her lip, she contemplated whether or not she should open it.

On the one hand, she'd had more than enough of him for one day. On the other hand, it could be important. He didn't usually bother to message her when he could come to see her at any time. He had once told her he felt phones were too impersonal for him.

Mindset for an emergency, she opened the message and almost fell to the floor in shock. There were many things she expected from him. Some accident had happened. Or a long-winded apology. Maybe even an attempt to start their argument again, but what had never crossed her mind was the image of his long, hard cock covering her screen.

She licked her dry lips and glanced away. And then looked at it again. Jason's hand was wrapped around the base as he held it out as if offering it to her. The tip glistened with precum that made her insides ache to clean it off.

Gulping and in sudden need of a cold shower, she closed her phone and set it back down. She didn't get more than a step away when it buzzed again. She knew it was Jason. He wouldn't send that kind of picture without wanting some sort of follow up.

Which she wasn't going to give him. But there was no reason not to watch him beg for it. Right?

Picking the phone back up, she prepared herself for what was sure to be an arrogant message asking her how she liked his present. But once again, she found herself dumbfounded to see a video message waiting for her. Before she could think about it, her finger pushed the play button, and Jason showed up on the screen.

This time, he was seated on a couch that she knew was in his apartment, her body was well acquainted with his black sofa. What wasn't familiar was the image of a clearly drunk Jason as he tried to hold the camera and stroke his length at the same time.

"See what you do to me?" His voice was gruff but slurred as he slid his hand up and down his shaft. "How hard you make this for me? I close my eyes and all I can picture is you."

Isabel's heartbeat rose and her panties soaked as her eyes locked on the movements of his hand. She knew she shouldn't watch. She should just delete the video and pretend like it never happened. Or better yet, bitch out Jason for sending it to her. But for the life of her, she couldn't make herself close it. She wanted, no, needed to see how it ended.

Jason grunted and his hand sped up, signaling his need to cum. She knew the tightening of his brow and the way he would bite his lip to try to keep from coming too soon all too well. It was a point she used to love to bring him also. Nothing got her off more than bringing this large, strong man to his knees, and watching him do so while thinking of her wasn't any different.

"Oh, sugar. I can't wait to be inside you again. To have your smart mouth wrapped around my cock." His breathing increased and his hand holding the phone shook, making it harder to see. When he came, he came hard, groaning her name, and then the screen turned black.

Seated on the bed where she had sat down during the video, she lowered the phone. Lying back on the mattress, she tried to calm the raging hormones screaming at her to touch her aching clit. Watching your ex get off to you was one thing, but masturbating to it was altogether another story. She already felt guilty enough as it was just watching the video.

She desperately needed that cold shower now. Turning her phone off, she moved to the bathroom but stopped when the sound of Vincent's voice coming from the end of the hall reached her ears. Was he home early?

Her raging hormones immediately cooled when she realized what she had just done. She shouldn't be reading text messages from her ex. What would she have done if Vincent had walked in?

Vincent and her hadn't done more than kiss. It still didn't give her an excuse to be having these thoughts. Isabel should be focusing on her current boyfriend and how he could get her hot. Maybe he was just waiting for her to make the first move? If that were the case, she was going to make that move right now.

WHEN SHE ARRIVED at Vincent's office, she found him on the phone. She crept in and leaned against his desk while she waited for him to finish. Vincent was muscular like many werewolves tended to be, with light brown hair and a face that was more on the feminine side than masculine. To any other woman, his features would have been strange, but she found him beautiful.

He smiled at her waiting figure and ended his call, his arms stretched out to her.

"Belle, my love, I'm so happy to see you." His words always well thought out, showed his strength and intelligence.

Letting herself be enveloped in his arms, Isabel breathed him in. He smelled like cinnamon and the woods, a smell that was distinctly him. She could curl up and fall asleep in that smell alone.

"What are you doing here? I thought you weren't coming home until tomorrow?" She leaned back from him to ask.

Kissing her forehead, Vincent's grin widened. "My last appointment was canceled at the last minute, so I flew back here as soon as I could. Did you miss me?"

"Yes." She fiddled with the buttons of his shirt, peeking up at him from under her lashes. Now was the time to show him how much. "Want to see?"

With a curious look on his face, he allowed her to lead him to the couch. Setting one leg on either side of him, she straddled his lap and made sure to press her heat against him as she shifted her hips. Sliding her hands into the hair at the nape of his neck, she pressed her lips to his, urging him to open up to her.

Surprised by her actions, he didn't respond immediately, but soon enough, his tongue slid into her mouth, and his hand found its way into her hair. She rocked her hips against him, trying to find the release Isabel had been so desperate for the last few months. When it wasn't enough for her, she placed her hands on his belt, determined to get what she wanted from him.

"Wait." Vincent pulled back and placed his hands on hers. "Now wait just a moment, love."

"What?" She sat back confusion on her face. "Don't you want me?"

His eyes roved over her tank top and shorts, heat in his eyes. "Of course, I want you, but as much as I want to, we can't be together like that yet."

"Yet? Is it because we aren't married?" She prodded her brows furrowing. "I didn't think you were that traditional, but if it's that, just tell me. I won't get mad."

Brushing a thumb down the line of her jaw, Vincent pressed his lips to hers. "That is what I love so much about you, Belle. You do not judge me like those who live in town. You simply accept me the way I am. Fur and all."

His chuckle brought a small smile to her face, though she was still troubled by his refusal.

"I had hoped to have this whole matter cleared up before it came to this point, but I see that you are as voracious a woman as you are intelligent." She blushed at his words but urged him to continue. "I have been away more often than usual so that I can fulfill my pack responsibilities. Responsibilities that keep me from you and your bed."

"What kind of responsibilities?"

"As a regular pack member, it would not have been of any importance for me to take a human wife, but as the Alpha's only son. There are certain conditions that must be met." A sinking feeling cooled any lingering lust in Isabel's body.

"And what conditions are those?"

Placing his hands on the side of her head, he leaned her head down to kiss it. "Now, don't you worry about it. That is for me to settle. Why don't you tell me about the spreadsheets I noticed that seem to resemble Swiss cheese?"

Frowning at his change of topic, she placed her hand on his chest and pouted. "But aren't your problems mine too? I want to worry about you."

Vincent matched her frown with one of his own. "Believe me, my love. I am worrying enough for the both of us."

"Fine." Standing from his lap, she straightened her clothing out. "If you'll excuse me, I have some numbers to rerun." With that, she spun on her heel and made for the door. Her previous hormones now frustrated for an entirely different reason.

# CHAPTER 5

## *JASON*

POUNDING ON HIS door was the first thing he heard when he woke up the next morning. The second thing he heard was the jackhammer going wild in his head. What did he do last night?

Jason cracked his eyes open and searched around him. Thankfully, he was in his apartment and had apparently passed out on the couch. The last thing he remembered was stumbling home from the bar, trying to get Diana, the feistier of the sisters, to accept that he wouldn't be going back with her that night.

The banging on the door continued, and Jason dragged himself up from the couch, his phone dropping from his lap and to the floor. The screen came on, showing his text messages and one name at the top glared out at him, making him groan. He did not drunk text Isabel, did he?

Picking up his phone, he popped open the conversation, which showed he had not only drunk texted her, but he had made a fool of himself flaunting his hard on. Shoving the phone inside his pocket, he wondered if there was a hole big enough to swallow him. That was if the incessant knocking on his door didn't kill him first.

"Jason, get your lazy ass up. I want to go hunting before I keel over," his dad's voice called out from the other side of the door.

"That's not likely to happen in the next five years, let alone the next five seconds." Jason opened the door with a weak smile. "Hi, dad."

"Finally." His dad pushed passed him without waiting for an invitation. "Where's the coffee?"

Jason stepped back, shutting the door behind him. While ex-military himself, he was built the same as Jason, but in the last years, his father had somehow shortened, putting him almost half a foot shorter than his son. At nearly sixty, the black hair that used to match Jason's was now more gray than black, giving it a peppered look.

"I don't have any made yet." Jason headed for the kitchen, knowing his dad would give him an earful either way.

"Not made yet! It's already six o'clock." He gestured at the clock on the wall. "How are you going to go hunting without a good cup of Joe?"

Rubbing a hand over his face, he remembered it was Sunday. Ever since Jason came back from overseas, he and his dad would go out in the woods, whether rain or snow, duck or deer season. Sometimes they came back empty-handed, sometimes they didn't. The point of it was to get out of work-life and spend quality bonding time. Today, though, Jason could use a bit more bonding time with his pillow.

"I had a long night." He handed his dad a cup of coffee and then leaned against the kitchen counter. "Do you think you could amuse yourself long enough for me to take a quick shower?"

"Shower?" His dad took a sip of his mug, taking a moment to appreciate the taste. "Why would you need to do that? You are just going to get dirty again."

Jason shrugged, not really wanting to get into it.

The older man leaned in and took a whiff of Jason. "Woo wee. You smell about a hundred proof. You shoot a gun smelling like that and you are likely to blow us all up. You get yourself in the shower, and I'll tend to your coffeemaker. We'll leave when you are done."

"Thanks, dad." Jason patted him on the shoulder on his way out of the kitchen and headed to the bathroom. If there was one thing he knew would distract his father, it was a good cup of coffee. Lucky for Jason, he knew how to brew one mean cup of Joe.

FORTY-FIVE MINUTES LATER, Jason and his father were deep in the woods that surrounded their little town of Rollings. So far, they hadn't been able to catch a glimpse of any quarry, which was just fine with Jason since he really wasn't in the mood for a hunt. His mind was still on the text messages he sent Isabel the night before.

"What's got into you, son?" His dad nudged him with his elbow.

"What do you mean?"

"First, you get pass out drunk, stinking to high heavens, and now you are too distracted to notice when a good doe has just crossed our path. Sounds a bit off to me." His dad shouldered his rifle, stopping their trek through the woods.

"I'm just tired is all."

His dad hummed, not quite believing him, and then after a moment, said, "You know, I heard a rumor around town."

"A rumor?" Jason's brow rose. "Since when do you care about rumors?"

"When they have to do with my son's future happiness, of course!" He swung his rifle around in the air.

"All right, all right." He held his hand up to calm him down before he shot them both. "What's this rumor you heard?"

Brushing a hand under his nose, his father shifted from foot to foot in a bit of a nervous gesture. "How much do you know about werewolves?"

Jason smirked. "What does anybody know about sups in general? They aren't exactly forthcoming with their secrets." His dad watched him waiting for a real answer. "Oh, all right. Werewolves are like most shifters, they can shift from human to animal on a whim, even without a full moon. Though I heard they are pricklier around the full moon and less in control of their beast—"

"Right," his dad remarked. "And there is one thing that shifters all have in common, and that is they are pack driven. They are all about tradition and the good of the pack."

"So?" Jason shrugged. "What of it?"

"There's been talk. They're saying our local werewolf hasn't just been visiting his folks up north but securing his legacy and place in the pack." His dad's eyes locked on to him, trying to tell him something he just wasn't getting.

"You're going to have to spell it out for me, dad. I'm not sure where you are going with this." Jason shifted his rifle from one arm to the other, the thought of the hunt completely gone from his mind.

"Son, come on now. I thought you were smarter than that. How do animals secure their place in society?" His dad urged Jason to come to the same conclusion as him.

Jason's face scrunched up in thought. What was his dad getting at? The only sure way to hold one's pack was through brute force or an heir. Just then, a light flickered on in his head.

"You think he's trying to produce an heir? With Isabel?" Disbelief coated his words, the very thought of it so absurd and maddening he couldn't think straight. Isabel pregnant? Jason knew Izzy well enough to know he'd never get her back if she had another man's baby. She was too loyal to leave Vincent without just cause.

"Well, if it is not our Isabel, then he's certainly working on it with someone else. But you can't tell me that all this time they've lived together that this wasn't a possibility?" His dad sighed, "Look, son, either she's already pregnant or is well on her way. Either way, you need to decide if you want to be involved with that kind of drama. Is she worth it?"

There was no question.

Isabel was worth all the heartache, drama, and more. By not giving up the last nine months, Jason had proven that and more. But if she was pregnant, did he want to ruin any chances for her future happiness by trying to drive a wedge between her and the wolf?

He wished he had an answer.

# CHAPTER 6

## *ISABEL*

WITH VINCENT BEING unwilling to confide in her, Isabel did the only thing she could do. Call on her sisters for help.

"It's been a while, Isabel." Belinda, the middle sister, watched her with curious eyes as if trying to pick apart a puzzle. While Isabel might be good with numbers, Belinda was good at solving people. It was one skill Isabel needed right then.

"Lately, you only call us when you want something." Her oldest sister, Lisa, took a sip from her cup of coffee, her blue eyes locking onto Isabel. She had always been the most stoic of the three sisters. Mature beyond her years but blunter than Isabel was comfortable with.

"I know. I meant to drop by sooner, but things have gotten busy up at the house." Isabel fidgeted with her own cup, her eyes now on the table.

Both of her sisters lived in Saint Paul, only Isabel had moved out to Rollings with her dad a few years ago. Even only thirty minutes away, none of them could ever agree on a place to meet, so whenever they did visit, they always went to May's Diner. Kind of a dump but they had the best apple pie. The best part was there was a booth in the back that was secluded enough to have a private conversation without the busybodies eavesdropping. This was one of those times she didn't want to be overheard.

"Well, it's understandable. I can imagine Vincent keeps you quite busy." Belinda remarked, a small smile on her lips.

"Not busy in the way you think." Everyone assumed she and Vincent were going at it like bunnies. If they were, Isabel wouldn't be here now.

"Oh, really? That's hard to believe." Lisa pursed her lips. "If I had that kind of man around me twenty-four seven, I'd never leave the bedroom."

"That's what I wanted to talk to you about." Isabel let her eyes trail out the window, not sure how to ask her question.

"Go on then. We don't have all day. Michael is at daycare, and you know how much I hate letting those idiots watch him." Lisa rolled her eyes. "They spend more time with their eyes on their cell phones than on the children."

"I told you to just call Jaime if you weren't comfortable sending my nephew there. She would have been perfectly happy to watch him." Belinda nodded her head at Lisa.

"Like that would happen," Isabel's oldest sister growled.

Belinda's girlfriend, Jaime, was an artist and made her own hours. While convenient, Lisa didn't think an artist was any more responsible than those at the daycare. Lisa's idea of a good parent was a nanny cam and locks on anything and everything that could be put in her two-year-old's mouth.

"Anyways," Lisa turned the conversation back to Isabel. "What did you want to talk to us about?"

Isabel sighed, might as well get it over with. "Vincent and I haven't slept together yet."

There was a stunned silence all around their table, the sound of the diner in the background the only noise that reminded her that she had not gone deaf.

"Come again?" Belinda inquired, tilting her ear toward her as if she had heard her wrong.

"You heard me." She crossed her arms over her chest and sunk a little deeper into the booth.

Her sisters exchanged a glance, doing that mental communication thing she had never been able to pick up before Lisa leaned forward, her voice low, "Why not? You've been together for months now. How in all that time have you not jumped his bones?"

Isabel threw her hands up. "It's not from lack of trying. At first, I thought he was just trying to be a gentleman, so I didn't bring it up. But last night, I decided to make a move and just when things started to get hot and heavy all of a sudden, he stopped."

"Are you sure he's not." Belinda gave her a knowing look that Isabel knew all too well.

"No." She shook her head. "He is not gay."

"How do you know? Did he seem, you know, interested?" Belinda tried to keep the smile off her face as she popped her pointer finger up.

Blushing furiously, Isabel ducked her head down. "No. He seemed interested enough."

Dropping her hand, her sister shrugged. "Well then, maybe he was tired, or he wants to wait until marriage. Have you asked him?"

"Yes," she cried out louder than she meant, attracting the eyes of the rest of the diner. Looking back at her sisters, she lowered her voice, "I mean, yes, I asked him about it."

"And?" Lisa prodded.

"He said it's pack business."

Lisa leaned back, her face twisted in confusion. "Pack business? What does your sex life have to do with pack business?"

"Hell if I know. He said something about securing his place in the pack and told me not to worry about it. When I tried to get him to tell me more, he kept deflecting, treating me like a child who was in over her head."

"Didn't you have the same problem with Jason?" Belinda frowned.

Isabel glared at her sister.

This wasn't like Jason. He'd made it clear he wanted her barefoot, and pregnant, and taking care of the children while he had a career. Vincent, on the other hand, loved Isabel for her independence. But it didn't make a difference if he didn't trust her. How could they be together if they couldn't trust each other?

Lisa smacked Belinda on the arm. "Don't compare him to that buffoon. That guy only knows how to do one thing and that's stick his big foot in his big mouth." She paused and then smirked. "Well, two things."

Her sisters broke out into a fit of laughter. She would think she would have learned by now not to confide in her sisters when it came to her sex life. They were worse than a bunch of gossiping grannies when it should be a serious matter.

"It's not funny."

"Of course, it's not, Isabel." Belinda wiped a tear from her face. "But what do you want us to do? We can't read Vincent's mind. From what you've said and what I've seen of your man, he could very well be planning on marrying you or joining the circus." Her lips quirked up at the last bit. "Let's just hope he is planning the former and not the latter. If you want a straight answer, you'll just have to poke around on your own or you put your big girl panties on and make he tell you the truth."

Neither one of those options were appealing to her. Isabel had hoped her sisters' would have thought of something she hadn't thought of. Something that didn't include a confrontation or worse, breaking what little trust Vincent had in her. His money he trusted her with, but apparently, there wasn't much else.

Standing from the table, Isabel turned toward the door. "Well, thanks for nothing. I'll see you two later."

"Oh, come on, Isabel. Stay and chat with us." Belinda held her hand out to her, trying to get her to sit back down.

"I really can't." She shook her head. "I have a lot of work I need to get done, and I suppose a decision to make."

Her sisters gave her matching supportive grins and wished her luck, making her promise to let them know how it all turned out. She would have liked to know how it would turn out as well. That was until she walked out of the diner and right into the last man she wanted to see.

# CHAPTER 7
## *JASON*

"I DON'T HAVE time for you," Were the first words Jason heard the moment Isabel realized who she had bumped into.

"Well, that's just too bad." He couldn't help but poke fun at her. "Because I am in desperate need of your time."

"Like last night? No, thank you." She pushed passed him and onto the busy sidewalk. It was barely after nine and while there weren't as many people as there were on Saturdays, there were still enough to draw interested glances their way.

Jason's face broke out into a sly grin. "So, you watched it, did you?" He quickly trailed after her, nodding his head to the passer buyers on their way to Sunday church service.

"Yes. I mean. No." She stuttered, her face becoming red at the looks they were getting. "You shouldn't have sent it to me in the first place."

He shrugged. "Well, if it is any consolation, I was drunk off my ass."

"I figured that out, thank you."

An uncomfortable silence settled between them as they walked down the sidewalk toward where he figured was the beast's mansion. He didn't like the quiet. It made him overthink about what his dad said that morning, and he was afraid he was going to blurt it out without any kind of tact. So instead, he did what he did best.

"So, tell me, Izzy." He lowered his head toward hers, his voice barely a whisper. "Did I make you wet?"

Isabel shoved Jason away, a blush flaring across her cheeks. "No, you did not."

"Really, now?" He chuckled and slid an arm around her shoulders to pull her close, not caring they were being watched. "Because I remember you liking to watch very much. How during a particularly boring day, you would beg for me to send you little videos like that." His mouth was hot against her ear and he whispered into it. "I love seeing your fingers deep inside of you, getting all wet just from watching me rub my cock."

Jason grunted when her elbow connected with his ribs and he dropped his arm. Rubbing his side, he watched her glare at him, her hands on her hips, poised and ready for a fight.

"That was before. You can't expect the same reaction out of me now, drunk or not." Her eyes darted to the crowd they were drawing, and she promptly turned on her heel, making her way toward her destination.

Shooting a glower at the nosy people of Rollings, Jason plodded after her. She might pretend like he didn't affect her, but he knew differently. What he didn't know was if he even had a chance anymore. Was she so set on Vincent because she was having his child?

"Why are you following me?" She almost screeched at him when she saw him behind her.

"I wasn't done talking to you." He spoke in his normal voice now that they were out of the crowded town center and closer to where the mansion sat.

"I think I was the one who was done talking to you."

Jason couldn't help but watch the way her bottom wiggled back and forth as she stomped away from him.

Catching up to her, he placed his hand on her shoulder, making her stop in her tracks. "Please. No more teasing, I promise. I just need to know."

"Know what, Jason?" She shrugged his hand off, irritation pinching her face.

"If you're pregnant."

Isabel's mouth dropped open, seemingly dumbfounded by his words. She didn't answer for a moment, and he almost thought she wouldn't until he saw a hand swinging toward him. He caught it just before it landed on his face and brought it down between them.

"Let me go," she snapped, tugging on her hand.

"Not until you answer me." Jason tightened his grip on her hand, pulling her closer.

"I am not going to dignify that question with a response. You know how I feel about having children. I believe I made myself quite clear before when I said I didn't want children right now, if ever," she growled at him. "Why in the world would that change?"

Jason frowned and dropped her hand. "I thought maybe you'd changed your mind." He tucked his hands in his pockets, his shoulders hunched. "You know, for him."

"Whatever gave you that idea?"

He had the decency to look ashamed. "Dad said he heard there was a rumor going around about the mutt trying to secure his legacy, and of course, everyone thinks that means a kid."

"So, you thought I would just go and get myself knocked up to keep him in the line of power?" She shook her head at him.

Rubbing the back of his neck, he let out an aggravated sigh. "I don't know what I was thinking. Just the thought of you and him having a kid when I want so badly for it to be me, I kind of lost my head."

"I'd say," she snorted, and then sighed, placing a hand on Jason's arm. "Hey. If I were pregnant, you would know, and not just because of some silly rumor. My sisters would have a whole fucking parade letting the whole country know."

Jason's lips quirked up in response. Her sisters were known for being overdramatic. They had caused more than enough friction between the two of them on more than one occasion. He wished he could blame their breakup on them, but it was all him and the very thing they were talking about.

"Iz. About that day." He started but she held her hand up and fumbled in her pocket for her phone.

"Sorry I have to take this." She swiped her phone open and pressed it to her ear. "Hey, dad. No, no, I can talk." She glanced up at Jason and mouthed a sorry before dashing away, along with another missed chance at redeeming himself.

# CHAPTER 8
## *ISABEL*

WHEN ISABEL ARRIVED back at the mansion, she couldn't stop thinking about Jason. She was such a coward. The moment she heard him start that conversation again, the one she had been avoiding for almost a year, she panicked. As lame as it was, pretending to get a call from her dad had been her only solution. She had too many problems already on her plate to worry about easing his conscience. The main one was sitting in her office, going over the reports she had pieced back together.

"Hey." She smiled at Vincent when he looked up from the papers in front of him.

"Sorry, they are kind of messy. I had to redo them cause of a mouse incident."

"We should get some traps to be sure it doesn't happen again."

"Already did." Plopping down into the chair opposite her desk, she watched him. Head bent as he read over the numbers, his hair fell over his face causing a shadow to fall over it. She chewed on her thumb as she thought about what Jason had said.

Did Vincent really want her to have his child? They had talked briefly about her concerns regarding having children before but nothing serious. If he did need her to get pregnant for him to keep his power in the pack, would she even do it?

"You are staring, Belle." He placed his hands on the desk and locked eyes with her. "What is on your mind?"

"Why does the town think you are trying to get me pregnant?" She blurted out before she could stop herself and winced at her lack of tact.

"What makes them think that?" Vincent cocked his head to the side, looking as confused as she had been when she heard it.

"Something about securing your legacy?" Isabel watched his face to gauge his reaction.

Vincent barked out laughing. A reaction she had not been expecting. Denial. Anger. Even a small part of her thought it might be right. But he shook his head as if he really couldn't believe what she had just asked him.

"Why is that funny?" She frowned at him, not understanding how having a child was a joking matter. Did he not want children?

"I'm sorry, my love, but it is funny because to secure my legacy, my firstborn must be a werewolf, and for that to happen, both its parent must be werewolves." He moved around the table and gathered her hands in his, laying his lips on the tops of them. "You don't have to worry your little head about being pregnant anytime soon."

"So, you are not trying to secure your legacy?"

"Oh, I am." He nodded his head, and then his lips curved down in a frown. "And while the thought of my first born not being with the woman I love is distressing, I do know it is for the good of the pack." He brushed a hand down her hair in a comforting gesture. "In time, you will see that it will be good for us too."

Her thoughts reeled. Vincent's words came out foreign to her. Isabel's mind had trouble wrapping around what the man who supposedly loved her just said. He was trying to secure his spot, but she didn't have to be pregnant for it to happen. Why would his first born not be with her? How could his first born not be with her? Unless...

"You are saying you have to have a child with a werewolf?" Her voice was steady even though her insides were shaking.

"Yes," he said simply, and then continued when it was clear she was waiting for more. "All my family asks is the first born be pure, and then they will leave us alone. I will not have to be dragged into all the politics and other pack nonsense. I can stay here with you." He smiled down at her as if he hadn't just dropped a bombshell on her.

Pulling her hands away from him, she stood from her seat and stomped across the room. "So, you are telling me that all this time you have been gone, you've been looking for a mother for your child?"

"Not looking. Assigned. My father has already picked a suitable pack mate for me to procreate with. She is a good woman, a good Beta. You would like her." He followed after her, holding his hand out to her.

Taking a step back from him, she forced herself not to deck him in his smiling face.

Her voice was low and steady, though threatening in its tone. "Have you slept with her?"

This time, his smile dropped, and his brow furrowed. "Of course, why do you think I cannot be with you yet? We cannot take the chance that I impregnate you first. We will not have long to wait. Lesly is on fertility drugs, and we have high hopes that an heir will be produced before long."

"Lesly?" She gasped, the room becoming smaller by the moment.

All this time, he had been so distant toward her not because he was a gentleman, it was because he wanted to get what constituted as his mistress pregnant first. Isabel wanted to scream for him to shut up, shut up! She wanted to wrap her hands around his throat and squeeze tight until he stopped saying these horrible things to her.

"How dare you," she snarled, pointing her finger at his chest. "How dare you think I would be okay with this? That I wouldn't care that you are having sex with another woman, let alone having a child. In what world do you think we live in where that is all right?"

Vincent's eyes narrowed, and for the first time since she had been with him, he looked angry. His soft blue eyes flickered to a glaring yellow. When the tension in the room increased tenfold, Isabel had a brief sense of fear fill her.

"In a world where supernatural creatures have intermingled with society." Vincent stalked her like the very animal he was. "In one that I had thought would accept our ways without judgment. I thought I had found that in you. Perhaps I was wrong."

"You were," she growled, shoving him away from her. "You disgust me."

Faster than she could comprehend, Vincent was on her, her arm in his tight grip. "I disgust you?" He snarled at her, his teeth elongating before her. "It is I who should be disgusted. My own woman cannot keep her hormones in check, long enough not to go panting after her ex-lover."

Isabel gasped as he bent her arm at a painful angle. "What are you talking about?"

"You and that Neanderthal." Grabbing her by her hair, he jerked her toward him. "Did you think I wouldn't know? That I wouldn't notice the way your scent changed when he was near you, or hear you at night when you dream about him? Hmm?" He twisted her hair in his hand, causing a sharp pain at her roots and a twinge in her neck.

Guilt rode through her at his words. He had known all this time and said nothing? She thought she had hidden her lingering feelings for Jason so well. Still, she had been fooling herself, about Jason and about Vincent.

A defiant part of her roared its head at her. So what? Even if he did know it didn't make up for the fact that he had been cheating on her this entire time. She might have had naughty thoughts about her ex, and been tempted on more than one occasion, but at least she wasn't going behind his back.

"Whose fault is that?" She spat at him, fighting to get out of his hold even though it hurt her more. "You won't touch me, you barely kiss me. It's no wonder I would long for someone else who actually wants me. Unlike you, you spineless, dickless, mutt."

Crack.

The sound of his fist colliding with her face resounded in her ears. Her eyes watered and pain radiated through the left side, knocking her to the floor. He had hit her. She wouldn't have ever believed it were possible had it not just happened.

"No more," his voice was dark as he hissed down at her. "You will not see him, think about him, or even mention him ever again." His eyes were now full yellow, and the hairs on her arms prickled as he loomed over her. "You are mine, and we are going to be happy."

Happy? From where she sat, her hand cradling her face, the idea of being happy with this monster was far from her mind. The only thing she could think of was getting as far away from him as possible.

# CHAPTER 9
## *JASON*

THE FACT THAT Isabel wasn't pregnant floated through his mind all day. He didn't want to get his hopes up, but he couldn't help the swell of anticipation building in his chest. If she cared enough not to want to hurt his feelings, that had to mean something, right?

Placing the last of the bug repellant he was stocking on the shelf, Jason made his way back down the aisle and toward the front of the store. He nodded his head at a few of the town's older ladies who were loitering around the homemade jam. With the fall festival coming up soon, he wasn't surprised to see them in his shop.

"It's a crying shame," one of the ladies whispered to the other, just as he got close to them.

"Oh, I know!" The other responded, shaking her head. "The poor dear, she really needs some foundation to cover that up, those sunglasses aren't fooling anyone."

"She shouldn't need to be hiding anything in the first place!" The first one whispered back, viciousness in her voice.

"I knew that supe was bad news the moment he moved to town." The first one's companion nodded her head, pity on her face. "She should have stayed with our dear Jason and none of this would have happened."

The sound of his name caused him to stop in his tracks, spinning on his heels, he made his way toward them.

Seeing him approach, they tried to look busy reading the labels of his mother's jam, but he wouldn't be fooled. There was one thing Jason had learned in all his years living in Rollings, and that was they didn't say things like that in hearing distance for no reason.

"Where is she?" He crossed his arms over his chest, letting his size do all the intimidating.

The ladies didn't shy away and went so far as to smile at him, confirming to him they knew exactly what they were doing.

"Why I do believe I saw her heading toward Caver's, but I could have been mistaken." The first lady, whose name he couldn't care less about, gestured out the window.

"Thanks." He spun from them, throwing his apron at a surprised Peter and marched out the door without a goodbye.

Stepping out of the store, his eyes immediately landed on a brown head, trying to look as inconspicuous as possible as she walked along the sidewalk. She did indeed have a big pair of sunglasses covering her eyes. Though he couldn't see her eyes, he could tell she was searching around her as if she were afraid something or someone would jump out at her any moment.

She stood outside of Caver's like she couldn't make up her mind whether to go in or not and then with one last look around hurried off the sidewalk and into the bar. Seeing his Izzy with such fear in her heart made his insides boil. A vengeful fury gripped him; before he knew what was happening, he had crossed the street and had entered the bar.

Jason scanned the practically deserted room. His eyes landed on the back booth, where a brown head was ducked down.

Making his way toward her, his eyes took in the way she was hunched down in the booth, her eyes locked on the screen of her phone, where she was searching for something he couldn't tell. She already had a glass of whiskey in front of her, her drink of choice when she was upset. Jason placed his hands in his pockets and rocked on his heels.

"It's a little early to be drinking, don't you think?"

"What's it to you?" She didn't glance up from her phone and actually seemed to sink further into herself. He didn't like it. He didn't like it at all. Was his sweet, strong, Izzy reduced to a skittish fowl? He would kill the mutt for putting that look on her face.

"Nothing, I'm just a concerned citizen." He slid into the booth, not missing the way she inched her hands back toward her and away from him.

Placing his hands on the table, he tried to rein in his rage when he caught a glimpse of the bruising peeking out from behind the edge of her glasses. The ladies had been right, she was wasting her time trying to hide behind them. He tried to figure out how to get her to talk to him without scaring her off.

"Just a citizen, then?" She snorted. "Not a persistent ex?"

"Not unless you want me to be?" He kept his tone light and friendly.

"I have had just about enough of men in my life right now. You can be a duck for all I care." She downed her drink in one go, letting it slam onto the table in front of them.

His lips quirked up at her choice. A duck it was. "Well then, as a concerned feathered friend, do you want to tell me why you are wearing sunglasses inside?"

"I have a headache," she countered; even behind the glasses, he could see her eyes daring him to question her.

"I'd imagine I would too if I had a shiner like yours." He gestured to her face, not pretending to not notice it anymore.

Growling, she jerked her glasses off and locked eyes with him. What he saw made his blood simmer. The monster hadn't just hit her, he had made sure it hurt. The lid around her eye was swollen shut and the blood vessels busted, making the area on and around her eye a vibrant purple. He knew from experience it would take days if not weeks to heal damage like that.

"Where is he?" Jason snarled, his hands gripping the edge of the table. It was taking all that he had not to rip the town apart looking for the spineless mutt who dared lay his hands on his Isabel.

"At home, I would imagine." She shrugged, a dark look crossing her eyes. The look made his heart clench even more, and he swore from then on, he would never let that look cross her face again.

"I'm going to kill him." Jason stood from the table and made for the door but Isabel grabbed his arm, jerking him back.

"No." She shook her head. "You'll just get yourself killed. Besides, it's my problem. Not yours. I'll deal with it myself." The stern line of her lips told him she really thought she could, and while he knew she could take care of herself, the thought of her being near that creature was too much for him to handle.

"Like you did before?" His hand reached out and brushed a finger lightly against the bruise on her face. "What is to stop him from hitting you again?"

Pain crossed her face, and he was pleased when she leaned into his touch before pulling back. "Nothing, I suppose, but as long as I don't make him angry, I'm sure I can reason with him."

"Reason? With a werewolf?" Jason gave a dark laugh. "That's not going to happen."

"Well, I can't go back right now, anyhow." She frowned at him. "Not until I have a plan."

"Yeah. The plan is you get as far away from the mutt as possible and let me put a bullet in that bastard's brain." Jason kneeled down next to her, cupping her hands in his. "You may not want me anymore but that won't stop me from keeping you safe. Please, let me do this for you."

"You'd really shoot him?" She quirked a brow at him.

"In a heartbeat."

"Fine." She pulled her hands away and pushed out of the booth, placing her glasses back on. "But we need a plan. You can't just go in there, guns blazing. Besides, I hardly think the Council for Supernatural Complaints would agree that death is a suitable punishment for domestic abuse."

"I don't give a fuck what the council would think," Jason snarled, pulling her to him. "You are worth so much more than that."

"That's sweet of you to say." She gave him a small smile. "But pretty words won't make that bastard pay."

# CHAPTER 10
## *ISABEL*

IT WAS AFTER midnight when they finally settled on a plan. They both decided that while killing Vincent would be satisfying, it wasn't exactly legal, or going to make their case any better. The big issue was whether or not the debt Vincent had forgiven when they had fallen for each other was going to be back in full effect when she left him.

Her father had a known gambling problem and had racked up over half a million dollars in debt at Vincent's little casino. How he had done it was beyond her, but she had been the dutiful daughter and tried to help her retired father out, which was how she ended up working for Vincent in the first place. She and Jason thought it would be prudent of her to let her father in on her plan, so he wouldn't have any surprises, and for him to prepare for the worse if Vincent did decide to collect.

"You should stay here," Jason tried to convince her, he seemed afraid to let her walk through his door and out of his life again. Not that she could blame him, tonight was the longest they had been in each other's presence in a long time, and it wasn't just him who was feeling reluctant to separate.

"I can't. I already told Lisa I would be staying over, and I'm already going to get an earful for being out so late." She shoved her things in her pockets, gathering her purse.

"All the more reason to stay." He had his hands in his pockets and was looking at her through his lashes with that little insecure boy look that had always been her Achilles heel.

"You don't even have a spare room," she pointed out.

"I'll sleep on the couch."

"Your couch isn't that comfortable." Their little back and forth was interrupted by the sound of her phone buzzing again.

For the last few hours, it had been going off nonstop with calls and messages from

Vincent, wondering where she was and when she was coming home. When she didn't answer the first few, the threats began. She had turned her phone off after that and had only recently turned it back on now that she was leaving.

"You shouldn't go out on your own right now. Stay here, I'll stay on the couch." He placed his hands on her shoulders, his lip quirked up on one side. "I promise to be the perfect gentleman."

Isabel bit her lip. She knew she should say no, to insist she go to her sisters. Being with him the last few hours had brought up all the feelings she had been trying to keep buried. Then there was the way he was looking at her now. The same way he used to when they were together. Like she was the only one in the room, and it made Isabel's skin sing, and it impossible to say no.

"All right." She let herself be led from the living room and into the bedroom she knew all too well.

Jason's bedroom was like him, rugged and wholesome. His bed was king size to hold his massive form, something she had always teased him about before. Now looking down at it, knowing she would be sleeping there without him gave her a weird sort of sadness. It seemed wrong somehow, but she couldn't bring herself to ask him to stay.

"I'll just take this pillow." He grabbed one from the bed and then the throw blanket at the end of the mattress.

"Um," she started as he made his way to the door. "I don't have anything to wear to bed."

Jason paused and looked her over, undressing her with his eyes, telling her exactly what he wanted her to wear to bed. After a moment, he went over to his dresser and pulled out one of his shirts, tossing it to her. Catching it in her arms, she forced herself not to bring it to her nose and breathe it in.

"Thank you," she muttered, her eyes never leaving his.

"If you need me, just holler." Jason's eyes smoldered as he watched her until the very moment the door closed between them.

YELLOW GOLD EYES stared out at her from the shadows. Her heart pounded in her chest as she backed away from them, trying not to draw attention to herself. A twig snapped beneath her foot and the muzzle to those eyes let out a growl. The sound of it made her bolt for the trees, the beating of her footsteps rung in her ears as well the four paws hitting the ground behind her.

The bushes scratched at her legs, bare but for the t-shirt that hung down to her knees. Fear gripped her and her lungs burned; she didn't dare look behind her, knowing he was right on her tail. She pushed passed the panic and pain in her lungs until her foot caught on a branch, and she spiraled down and down.

Falling onto the ground, it didn't take long for him to be on her, snarling and snapping at her. She cried out and gripped the fur in front of her, trying to push him off. She locked her arms in front of her, pressing it against his throat as his sharp teeth snapped at her. All of a sudden, the wolf above her turned from animal to human—muzzle to jaw.

The blonde head of Vincent sat above her, no longer biting at her, but pushing her hands down beside her as she struggled. Laughter sounded in her ears as she fought to get him off until she jerked awake when the door to the bedroom flew open.

"Izzy," Jason's voice cried out to her, and her eyes looked to his silhouette in the doorway, the light from the window barely enough to distinguish his features.

Her breathing was labored as she tried to calm herself. It was only a dream. Vincent couldn't get to her here. Not while Jason was there.

"I'm okay," Isabel gasped, her words hoarse. "It was only a bad dream."

"You're safe here, Izzy. I won't let him hurt you." Jason stepped forward and then stopped thinking better of it.

"I know." Isabel looked down at her hands, the dream still making them shake with fear.

"Well then, I guess I'll just go." He pointed a thumb back behind him, and half turned to leave.

"Stay."

Before she could stop herself or even think about it, the single word fell out of her mouth. A word that caused Jason to pause in the doorway. Her eyes locked onto him and waited for him to comply with her request.

"Are you sure?" He stepped into the room, the moonlight landing on his shirtless chest, making her mouth go dry.

Gulping, she nodded her head and then licked her lips.

"I'm not going to apologize, Izzy." His feet padded on the carpet as he made his way toward her. "I'm not always going to say the right thing. I won't always make the right choices." He stopped in front of her, the waistline of his boxers at her eye line. "I am not the smartest man. I know what I want and what I want is you. But don't ask me to stay with you unless you are ready to deal with the consequences. I won't lie next to you like a good boy and keep my hands to myself. I'm not that kind of man. If I'm going to stay with you, I sure as hell am going to be buried deep inside of you."

His words caused a bit of anger to flare, but it was trumped by the aching need she had for him between her legs and in her heart.

She knew what asking him to stay would mean, and every part of her screamed at her not to care. So, what if he wasn't perfect? If they didn't have everything in common, what couple did? Isabel was tired of fighting, with him and with herself. She just wanted it to be like it used to be between them before the misunderstanding and Vincent.

So when she told him to stay, this time, her eyes locked with his. Isabel let all the words she wanted to say, all the emotions she had held back in the last nine months fill her up. Until it was clear that she wanted him and him alone.

# CHAPTER 11
## *JASON*

THE LOOK IN her eyes made his heart thud in his chest and his cock hard as a rock. In an instant, he was on her, one hand finding its way to the back of her head while the other wrapped one silken leg around his waist as he pressed her down into the bed. He couldn't believe he was actually here with her, getting to touch her like this once again.

He had thought about it sure. Before Izzy had called out, he had been torturing himself with different scenarios that would cause him to jump from the couch and end with her in his arms. But he had never imagined those things actually happening.

So, when he heard her cries of panic, his body was already up and through the door before he realized anything was wrong. Then when his senses came back to him, and he saw her there in his bed, in his shirt, all thoughts of comforting her went out the window, and all he wanted was her.

Isabel let out a soft sigh as she sunk into his embrace, letting him take the lead. His hand traced along the outside of her thigh, and he forced himself to go slow, to take his time. No matter how much he wanted to rip the clothes from her back and bury himself inside her.

It seemed like she was having the same problem he was, because she arched her hips into him, pressing her heat against the thin front of his boxer. She moaned when her clit came into contact with his hardened length, and it took all his willpower not to let her have her way.

But he had waited too long for this. Nine months was a long time to go without sex and he wanted this to last. Who knew what would happen in the morning? She could change her mind as women sometimes did and try to blame it all on being afraid and vulnerable. No. If this was the last time he ever got to feel her in his arms, it would be under his terms.

Leaning back from her so she could get the friction she needed, he almost smiled at the whine that came from her throat. His hands found their way under her shirt and pushed it up and over her head. Jason's eyes soaked in the sight of her.

He had always said that Isabel had the most perfect breasts he had ever seen. Just this side of a handful and so sensitive to his touch that his eyes boring down on them alone caused the nipples to harden.

"Jason," she moaned when he kept staring at her, not moving to touch her. "Please, touch me."

"Not yet," he murmured, his eyes trailing from her perfect breasts to her panties that were soaked where they pressed against her. His hand reached up and cupped her hips, sliding his hands underneath the edges of her panties before pulling them down, revealing her to him.

Isabel moaned and wiggled beneath his gaze. He could tell she was getting frustrated, that if he didn't touch her soon, she was going to go crazy, which was precisely how he wanted her. To want his touch so severely that she couldn't stand it, the same way she had made him feel for almost a year.

Jason leaned down, pressing his mouth against the skin between her breasts, savoring the taste of her against his tongue, but never quite touching the areas she wanted. He let his mouth leave a trail of hot wet kisses down her stomach and traced along the edge of her hip bone. He threw one leg over his shoulder and pressed his face between her thighs, not touching, just breathing against her.

"Jason. Please," she groaned, her hands finding their way into his hair, trying to push him to where she wanted him.

He loved to hear his name on her lips, especially like this. When she was begging for it, and he knew he was the only one who could give her what she wanted. When his tongue finally slipped out and lapped along her heated skin, she wailed at the contact and tried to close her legs around him.

Determined to keep in control, he used his strength to keep her open for him, circling and teasing her just short of her release. With each pant and moan of his name, his own arousal heightened, making it almost painful to deny himself much longer.

Isabel thrashed against him, trying to buck her hips up and closer to him. Instead of pulling away from her, he grabbed her hips and pressed his mouth against her clit and sucked hard. The sound of her howling in his ear made him slide his finger inside of her, making sure she was good and ready for him.

While she was still riding her high, Jason removed his mouth and aligned himself between her thighs. Pulling his boxers down, he thrust the full length of himself into her but stopped at the feel of her so tight around him.

"God, baby. Give me a moment," he gasped, not prepared for the overwhelming feeling of being inside of her. "So tight," he croaked out, almost blowing his load right there.

Wiggling her hips against him, this time, she made him whimper and beg. "It feels so good to have you inside of me again," she whispered in his ear, knowing her dirty talk always made him lose control. "It's been almost a year since I've had anything that didn't take batteries in me. It's just not the same."

Jason looked down at her for a moment, his brows crinkled. "You haven't with the mutt?"

A wicked smile crossed her face, and when she shook her head, it killed the last bit of his restraint.

Planting one hand above her, he used the other to get a good grip on her hip, pulling back and then driving into her, causing them both to gasp and moan. He had wanted to make it last but knowing the mutt hadn't touched her, hadn't been inside of her, made him throw all of his plans out the window. All he could think of now was bringing them both to a state of oblivion.

Isabel had other ideas.

While she had seemed perfectly content to let him be in control, it didn't last long before she hooked her foot around his leg, pushing him up and over until she was writhing on top of him. Each movement she made as she rose above him only to sink back down on his length caused a twinge in his heart. It sounded sappy even to him but at that moment the way she moved, the way she seemed so delighted to be with him was the most beautiful thing he had ever seen.

He placed his hands on her hips and helped her move against him, urging her to lean forward, so the top of her brushed against him. They moved like that for a few minutes, eyes on each other while each movement brought them closer to the edge. Before long, he felt his balls tighten, and he knew he wasn't going to last much longer.

Flipping them over again, he braced one hand on her hip. He slid the other between them, rubbing her bundle of nerves in rapid concession. A smirk of satisfaction slipped onto his face as he watched her mouth drop open, and her eyes roll back into her head. Only when her whole body tensed, and her insides clenched around him did he let himself go.

Jason slammed into her over and over, trying to make Isabel's orgasm last as long as possible while he reached for his as well. Each stroke along her insides made him grunt, and his legs quake, and when he was almost there, he leaned into her, his mouth brushing her ear.

"I love you, sugar."

To any other woman, those words would have been blown off as a man talking in the heat of the moment but not with Izzy. He knew from the way her eyes filled with emotion that she knew he meant it, and as sweet oblivion found them, he vowed never to let her go again.

# CHAPTER 12
## *ISABEL*

WHEN ISABEL WOKE the next morning, she felt a familiar weight on her back that made her smile. Last night's activities flashed through her mind. Thinking about the way Jason had touched her and how he remembered just how to make her beg caused a heat to pool in her stomach.

As if knowing she was thinking about him, a thick bulge pressed into her butt, and a large hand slid up to cup her breast. A smile crept onto her face and she wiggled her behind, loving the feel of him hard and warm against her. A low growl rumbled through Jason, causing her to giggle, only for her to gasp when his hand found its way between her thighs.

"Laugh at me, will you?" His sleep filled voice combined with his fingers on her clit threw her over the edge, panting his name.

As she came down from her high, she rolled over to look at him. Her finger traced the line of his jaw where stubble had begun to form, and her eyes trailed over his face while she tried to memorize each feature. She didn't know how she ever thought she didn't love this man. The very thought of it was ludicrous.

Letting her hand trail down his face and onto his chest, she pursed her lips. "So, what now?"

"Now?" He grabbed her around the waist and drew her on top of him. "I thought I'd take the day off to reacquaint myself with every inch of your delectable body."

Isabel moaned when he aligned himself to slide into her once more.

Placing her hands on his chest, she rocked against him, gasping and groaning as he rubbed along her aches from last night's lovemaking. Her nails bit into his skin, causing him to hiss. His hands directed her hips so that her clit rubbed against the front of him, while his cock tortured her inner walls.

Crying out as she found her release once more, she collapsed on top of him. Isabel snuggled into his embrace, his hand petting the top of her head. She wished she could lie there all day, but while she couldn't imagine anything better, there was still the issue of Vincent to deal with.

"What is it?" Jason's hand stopped when her body tensed.

She sighed and sat up. "I was just thinking about how we are going to deal with Vincent."

Frowning, Jason places his hands on her hips, his thumbs circling her skin. "We'll do what we planned. You will go talk to your dad, give him a heads up about what might happen and then afterward, we will go deal with Vincent together."

"What about us?" She tilted her head to the side, a little hesitant to bring it up.

Leaning up, he kissed her nose. "One problem at a time."

"All right but I'm still not sure you being there will help the matter." She moved off of his lap, his hands becoming too much of a distraction when she needed to think. "Especially if I smell like you."

"So what? Let him know." Jason grabbed her hips, pulling her back to him before she got too far away. "Let him know who you belong to."

Smirking at him, she caught his hand before he could slide it between her thighs once more. "And who would that be?"

"The most eligible bachelor in town, of course." He gave her his megawatt smile. "I have heard I am quite a catch."

"Oh, is that so?" She quirked an eyebrow at him. "I heard you are nothing more than full of hot air."

"If I'm full of anything, it is love for you." Jason leaned down and nipped at her nose, causing her to rub at it.

Isabel laughed and then sobered at his words. That was twice Jason had told her he loved her in the span of a few hours and once that wasn't during sex. Isabel knew she loved him. She always had. Still, Isabel couldn't bring herself to say the words, not yet.

"I have to get ready to talk to my father." She eased out of his arms, pretending to ignore the frown on his face. "I'm going to take a shower and I suppose." She looked around the room for yesterday's clothing. "I'll have to be that girl today."

"That girl?" He moved to the edge of the bed, not caring that he was nude and giving her an eye full.

She gulped and turned to grab her clothes, her need for him even more now that she had just had another taste of him.

"You know, the walk of shame girl. Wearing last night's clothes, just fucked hair, and ruined makeup?" She explained her hands moving wildly in the air as she picked up her clothes.

"Oh, that girl." Jason nodded his head, not hiding the pleased smile on his face. "Well, if you take a shower, you will just look like the girl who slept in her clothes rather than the just fucked girl, though I wouldn't mind it in the least."

Isabel snorted. "Of course, you wouldn't. But I still need to shower, and you need to get dressed if you are going to help me storm the castle today."

"Or we could shower and then after you talk to your father, storm the castle together." Jason stood from the bed, his long muscular legs approaching her fast.

Eyes locked on the glorious sight he made, she let the clothes fall from her hands. "Or we could."

SEVERAL HOURS LATER than she wanted, Isabel found herself standing outside her father's house. A small two-bedroom with shuttered windows and a small patio, it had been her house not too long ago before Vincent had insisted she move into one of his guest bedrooms.

She didn't know how she had ever let herself be convinced into leaving. She loved her father's house and had been vehement with Jason about waiting until they were married before she ever moved out. Not just for her benefit but for her father's, who didn't have much going for him nowadays.

Walking up the front porch, she paused outside the door, not sure if she should knock or just enter. While she tried to decide, her father made up her mind for her by opening the front door, a surprised look on his face that when he got a load of her eye turned into an angry frown.

"What in the hell happened?"

"Hi, daddy." She gave a weak smile, her head ducked down.

"Well, don't just stand there, come on in." Her father opened the door wider and gestured her through. "Then you can tell me what man thought they could lay a hand on my daughter."

Taking a seat in the living room, Isabel watched her father move through the house. Short like her, his hair was completely gray, as were his beard and mustache. He was stocky through the middle and had a bad cough most days from smoking too much in his younger years. Pushing seventy, she was surprised he had lasted this long without needing a nurse around.

"I like what you've done with the place." She gestured to the new paint that hadn't been there last week, a kind of white green that really did nothing for the beige furniture.

"Now, don't be trying to distract me." He waved a hand at her, his eyes narrowed on her bruised eye. "Who hit you? That mutt?"

Her father never did approve of her going to work for Vincent, not to help him or for any reason. When he found out she was dating him, he about had a heart attack. There was one thing her father and Jason had in common, they both didn't care for sups, but at least Jason was more tactful about it. Her father, well, he could be a bit harsh.

"I told you he was trouble and you should stay away from him, didn't I?" He wagged a finger at her when she didn't answer his question.

"I was only trying to help. How were you going to pay back the money without it?" Isabel reminded him.

"I would have found a way," he grumbled, crossing his arms over his chest. "It was my problem, and I should have dealt with it, not you. I wish I'd never stepped foot in that damned place, then you would have never met that miserable wolf."

Isabel sighed, there was no reasoning with him when he got like this. He could go on for hours and hours and she would never get out what she came to say.

"I was coming to talk to you about that actually." She touched her eye briefly, the area still tender. "I found out some rather unpleasant news about Vincent and plan to break up with him."

"On your own?" Her father jumped up from his chair. "After he already hit you once? I won't have it! I'm coming with you."

"Now hold on a second." She moved from her seat and placed a hand on his arm before he could march out the door. "Jason is already going to be my backup, so you can just sit back down."

"Jason, you say?" Her father's eyes lit up. "Well, why didn't you say so? He's such a great guy. I don't know why you two ever split up."

"That's another thing I wanted to talk to you about." Isabel sat back down, her hands fiddling in front of her. "The reason Jason and I broke up was because he wanted children, and well, I don't. Or I didn't."

"When did this happen?"

"I've always felt that way, ever since mom left." Isabel glanced at the wall, her eyes pricking with tears.

"Oh, Isabel." Her father sat down next to her on the couch, taking her hands in his. "That had nothing to do with you." He sighed, weariness in his voice. "She never wanted to settle down, have kids. She wanted to travel the world. But when Lisa was born, she tried, she really did. She loved you and your sisters but she let it tie her down. Your mother didn't see how she could ever have both, and when it came down to it, she decided she couldn't be the best mother for you if she couldn't be the best of herself."

"Isn't that being selfish? Don't you hate her for it?"

"I did for a long time." He turned to her and held her shoulders. "But that doesn't have to be you. Having kids does not have to be the end of your dreams and ambitions; you can have it all and be happy. You just have to choose to make it happen."

Isabel smiled and hugged him. "Thanks, daddy. That's what I needed to hear." Standing from the couch, she moved for the door.

"So, are you two back together then?" He asked, causing her to stop at the door.

"We'll see." She gave him a wink and stepped out onto the porch.

As she left her father's house, she couldn't help the sense of relief that fell over her. She wasn't her mother. Nothing was stopping her from being happy. Or so she thought.

"Hello, Belle."

# CHAPTER 13
## *JASON*

EVER SINCE ISABEL left the apartment, Jason couldn't stop smiling. It had come to the point where he was scaring his customers away, and he had to force his jaw to relax.

"You look happy." Lu leaned against the shop counter, watching Jason with a knowing grin on his face.

"Well, I am," he said over his shoulder as he rearranged some of the products on the front counter. He wasn't going to let his friend's teasing ruin his good mood. He had Isabel back and the wolf almost out of the picture. Nothing could go wrong.

The other man chuckled and adjusted the utility belt of his police uniform. "And that wouldn't have anything to do with you and Isabel leaving the bar together yesterday, would it?"

"Possibly." Jason couldn't keep his lips from curving up once more. He wasn't surprised that they had been seen. They hadn't been trying to hide it, and a small part of him hoped everyone in town saw her leave his apartment that morning as well.

"So, are you back together or what?"

That made Jason's smile fall a bit. He didn't know what was going to happen between him and Isabel. Once things were settled with the mutt, he had hoped they would start back up where they left off. Though, he couldn't help but notice the three little words that had yet to pass through Isabel's lovely lips. He had no doubt that she loved him, but if it was her that needed to admit it.

"We'll see." Jason placed the last of the displays on the counter. "But that's not what I called you over here for."

"Oh, yeah? So, you didn't just want to gloat and say I told you so?" Lu quirked a brow at him. "Now, that's not like you at all."

"Not today, at least. I have a bigger problem to deal with." Jason sighed, running a hand through his hair. "Short of killing the bastard, I don't know how to get the mutt out of town and out of Isabel's life. I just don't see him leaving on his own, not after the way he hit her before."

Lu looked down at his hands in thought. "Well, the problem is right now all you have on him is domestic abuse. Isabel could press charges against him and get a restraining order. Still, frankly, with his dad being the Alpha of the state, I don't see any charge sticking to him long."

"That was what I was afraid of." Jason placed his forearms on the counter, racking his brain for some way to get him out of their lives forever when his phone rang.

Digging it out of his pocket, he saw it was Isabel's dad. Confusion covered his face as he swiped open the call and placed it to his ear. "Frank, how are you? Did Isabel make it over there all right?"

"I'm fine." Frank's voice a bit harsher than he thought it would be. "What isn't alright, is that mutt who just grabbed Isabel from my front yard."

"What?" Jason gripped the counter, his eyes looking to Luis, who had tensed up at his panicked look. "Vincent took her? When? How?"

"Not five minutes ago. Knocked her clean out! I'd have gone after the bastard myself had he not been so damn fast." The anger in Frank's voice could be felt over the phone, and Jason didn't blame him, he was having a hard time keeping it together himself.

"Why didn't you call the police?" Jason looked to Lu, who had started talking into his radio.

"I figured with you being buddies with most of them, you'd be better at getting them riled up and ready. No one really listens to an old fuddy-duddy like me anyways."

"Will do. Don't worry, Frank. I'll get our girl back."

"I know you will, just don't get yourself killed in the process or she'll end up dating a bloodsucker, or worse, a fae." Jason almost smiled at the shudder that was sure to have gone through the older man. Most people had come to accept the supernaturals but a lot of the older folks, Isabel's father included, were still stuck in their ways.

"Well, we can't have that," Jason remarked and hung up the phone. He threw off his work apron, locked the register. Grabbing his rifle from underneath the counter, he headed for the door with Lu tight on his tail.

"I called in a kidnapping with a history of domestic abuse," Luis explained, bringing Jason over to his car.

"That won't light a fire under them!" Jason complained, slamming the door of the car, as Luis flipped on the lights and siren.

"Don't worry, it will." He smirked at his friend. "I told them it was Vincent."

Setting the rifle between his legs, Jason tightened his hold on it. With Vincent being a werewolf that not only put him in the category of the supernatural crimes but the armed and dangerous category. Werewolves were the worst kind of supes to get mixed up with, unpredictable and overemotional. Those humans who dared to love them usually ended up in Isabel's position, or worse, dead.

# CHAPTER 14
## *ISABEL*

BOUND AND GAGGED, Isabel watched as Vincent paced back and forth across the floor. When she had heard his voice outside her father's house, she'd about two seconds to panic before a fist came flying at her face once more. Body aching and lip split, she had been brought to Vincent's office, and the moment she woke up, she'd tried to run.

She got the door open when she came face to face with Vincent waiting on the other side. He had taken one unsurprised look at her and dragged her back into the room. That was when he trussed her up like a Thanksgiving turkey and left her lying helpless on the floor.

"Ah, my Belle. Why do you do this to me?" Vincent stopped next to her, squatting down to take in her position. "We could be so happy, you and me. If you would just do as you are told."

Isabel glared up at him and tried to tell him no fucking way through the gag biting into her mouth. The crazy werewolf still thought they had a chance together. She was insane to believe talking to him would have fixed everything. Nothing short of a silver bullet was going to make him let her go.

"I hate seeing you like this, my love." He brushed a hand down the side of her face and she jerked away from his touch. "I would have preferred when I tied you up it would be for our equal pleasure not to keep you from leaving."

The very thought of him touching her made her stomach roll. It was funny in a sad way that just days before, she was begging for his touch. Now, she wanted to cut his hands off so he would never put his filthy paws on her again.

Bending down until he was eye level with her, Vincent's eyes glowed the golden yellow of his wolf form. She inched away when his nose buried into the base of her neck, a low rumbling growl filling his chest as he breathed in her scent. Before she knew what was happening, she was thrown onto her back, her hands shoving into the middle of her spine as Vincent loomed above her.

"You couldn't wait to get back to him, could you?" He snarled, his teeth elongating and his face becoming more wolf than man. "Did you need a cock that badly?"

Isabel cried out when his clawed hands dug into her hair, dragging her face up to his. His hot breath blew across her face and she tried to talk through her gag.

"What was that, my love?" His voice had transformed into a deep gurgling sound as if it was hard for him to speak.

Isabel jerked away from him and tried to get the words out around the gag, but they only came out as a bunch of muffled noises.

"Ah, this is in the way." Vincent slid a claw beneath the gag, pausing with it just against her skin. "If I take it off, will you promise not to scream? You will speak like the intelligent adult you are?"

Trying to keep the hate out of her eyes, she sighed and nodded her head, careful not to let the sharp edges of his nails scratch her face. The last thing she wanted was to be a werewolf, who knew what the local pack would do if that happened.

"Good girl."

The moment Vincent's claw sliced through the fabric, Isabel screamed as loud as she could, hoping someone, a servant or someone passing by, would hear her pleas for help. Before she could catch her breath to scream again, Vincent's paw flew out and wrapped around her throat, cutting her breath off mid-gasp.

"That was uncalled for, Belle." His hand gave her a little squeeze as she struggled against his grip. "You promised not to scream, and you did it anyway. How am I to trust you if you do not keep your word?"

Isabel felt like she was dying. Her lungs burned, and her eyes began to water, she couldn't breathe. She could feel the edges of her mind start to blacken when his grip loosened, allowing her to take in shaky rapid breaths.

His hand still on her throat, he watched her drag in breath after painful breath, the pad of his thumb stroking the column of her throat. Vincent seemed to be unfazed by her pain, but the glint in his eye and the quirk of his lips as she glared up at him told her he was indeed getting some pleasure from her suffering.

"Now, let us try this again." He used the hand not holding her throat to move down the length of her body, caressing her as if they were lovers about to make love. When his hand reached the apex of her thighs, she suppressed a whimper and almost sighed in relief when he did nothing more than brush against her before ripping the restraints at her ankles.

With her legs free, she immediately tried to kick out but he was ready for her. He grabbed her thigh and pushed himself between her thighs, successfully removing all hope of causing him any significant damage.

"Isn't that more comfortable?" His hand traveled its way back up her body, and she tried not to cringe when she felt his hardened length as it rubbed against her. He grabbed Isabel's bound hands, and she had a small moment of hope that he would release her, and she could get away. But all he did was tug on them, so her back arched into him, and panic filled her again.

Removing his hand from her throat, he cupped her breast in his hand, rolling her nipple through the fabric. "You are such a beautiful woman, Isabel. You have no idea the torture it has been for me to keep away from you all these months. I had hoped when we finally came together, we would equally be aching for the other." His fingers pinched down hard, causing her to cry out. "You must understand my disappointment to find the woman I love does not crave me in return."

"I'm sorry to disappoint you." Isabel croaked out, trying to keep him talking and not focused on touching her.

"Oh, but you did, my Belle. You wounded me in here." He pressed his palm to his heart, a sad smile on his face.

"I never meant to hurt you," she whispered, her throat hurting too much to do much else.

"I know. I know. And if I am truthful, I am partially to blame." He combed a hand through her hair, petting her the way he used to. "If only I had told you about our custom beforehand then you would have been prepared for it. It was hardly fair that I was able to relieve some of my aches for you through Lesly, but you had no relief in return."

"It's all right." Her breath came in small pants, unsure of where he was going with his words but afraid to do more than pretend it was okay.

"No, it's not." He shook his head, the gesture looking strange and out of place on his half human half wolf face. "You were suffering, and I did nothing to soothe it. The one time you came to me to ease your pain, I pushed you away rather than offering up an alternative. But not this time."

Isabel made a small noise when without warning, he shredded the front of her clothes, exposing her breast and panties to him. A low growl filled him as his eyes ran across her bare chest. Somehow being naked in front of him was so much worse than being tied and beaten.

Licking his jaws, Vincent bent down to lap at her skin. Isabel held her breath as she felt his tongue slide along the valley of her breast and moved to wrap around her nipple. He sucked it into his mouth before popping it back out with a grin.

"We may not be able to consummate our love yet, but that does not mean I cannot make you feel pleasure." His hand slid down to the waistline of her panties, dipping his fingers into touch her there. "And I'm going to make you feel so good, my love. My Belle."

Gulping down the bile building in her throat, Isabel nodded. If she couldn't get away, then she just had to stay alive long enough for Jason to find her. There was little doubt in her mind that someone in this small town hadn't seen Vincent take her. If she could stay alive and bide her time, someone would come. They had to.

# CHAPTER 15
## *JASON*

WHEN LUIS' SQUAD car pulled up in front of the mansion, it was quiet. There were no cars in the driveway, no neighbors walking their dogs. It was as if they knew to stay away.

Jason didn't like it. It was too quiet. His poor Izzy, what was he doing to her?

Stepping out of the car, he placed his rifle in his hand, ready and willing to blast the bastard back to where he came from.

"Woah there, Jay." Lu held his hands up. "You have to at least pretend that you aren't planning on shooting him. You don't want to get arrested for premeditated murder."

Growling at his friend's words, he lowered his rifle. He didn't give one fuck about getting arrested, if that mutt so much as placed another finger on her, he would blow him away.

"Fine. Let's go." He started up the walkway Luis in tow.

"We really should wait for back up before we go in guns blazing," Luis whispered to him. "You never know what could be behind that door. There might be more than one werewolf we are dealing with, you know."

"We can't wait for them to finish pussyfooting around. My girl is in there, and I am not going to sit here while that bastard does God knows what to her." Jason stepped up to Luis, his face inches from his. "Now, are you with me or not?"

"Always." Luis smiled at him, unsnapping his gun from its holster.

"All right." He nodded his head, his hand on the door of the mansion. "When we get in there, we should keep an eye out for civilians we don't want to shoot any innocent bystanders, though, from the looks of the place I'd say the mutt was smart enough to clear it out."

"Hey, I'm the officer here, shouldn't I be in charge?" Luis stepped up, trying to take the lead.

Jason smirked at him before pushing him aside. "We might be discharged but I'm still your superior."

"Whatever you say, Sergeant." Lu gave him a one-finger salute before moving back from the door. "Let's go get us a werewolf."

Jason threw the door open, sweeping the room with his rifle, and then relaxed when no one came out. Inching his way into the foyer, he kept his eyes open for any servants that may be around. Gesturing to Luis to cover him, he moved around the edge of the entrance and entered the hallway.

There were several doors and still no sign of anyone. Jason crept up to the first door and locked eyes with Lu before throwing the door open, his rifle sweeping the room. When it turned out to be just an empty bedroom, they proceeded to do the same routine with three other doors, which also turned out to be bedrooms.

Jason was losing patience and was about to just start yelling Isabel's name when a strangled cry came from the end of the hall. Feet moving on their own, he hurried toward the sound. Without waiting on Luis, Jason kicked open the door.

The moment the door opened and revealed Vincent with his back to him, Jason's rifle was on him. Racking the slide of the gun, he stepped into the room, his eyes searching for Isabel petite form.

"Where is she, mutt?"

Vincent turned his head half toward him, causing Jason to pause. He had never seen a werewolf in half-wolf form. Leering yellow eyes glowered at him above the snout that was in the place of his nose. His teeth were more fangs and were sharp enough to make Jason stop and think.

Luis came up behind him, a shocked gasp falling out of him.

"She is where she belongs, human," his voice was raspy and snarled as he snapped his chomps at them. "You should not have intervened."

"Where she belongs is with me. Now I'll ask you once more before I put a bullet in your sorry excuse for a hide. Where is Isabel?" A muffled whimper came from where Vincent was still kneeling down, his massive form hiding whatever was behind him.

The chance that the whimper was from Izzy caused rage to burn through Jason.

Before Luis could stop him, he charged forward at the werewolf, his gun ready to blast him in the face. Vincent spun around and swiped his legs out from under him before he was able to get a shot off.

Back hitting the ground hard, knocking the wind out of him, Jason fought to catch his breath. Luis jumped over him, his gun drawn and pointing at the wolf.

"You don't want to do this, man," he tried to reason with him. "You already have kidnapping and assault charges; you don't want to add murder to it."

Jason crawled to his knees and then to his feet, searching for his gun as Luis kept Vincent distracted. He found his rifle next to a half-naked Isabel, who had tears in her eyes and a wad of cloth shoved into her mouth. Forgetting the gun, Jason could only focus on getting Isabel out of there.

He scrambled across the floor and knelt at her side, pulling a knife from his boot. Sadness and anger covered his face at the way the wolf had her tied but was relieved to see her panties still on her body. Pulling the gag from her mouth, he cut the restraints on her hands. He tried to ask her if she was alright when he was knocked away. But this time, when he fell, he kept a hold of his weapon.

Spinning back around, he looked for Lu, who was out cold on the floor near the door. Eyes locking back onto the monster, who was standing in front of Isabel as if he had to protect her from him. Almost laughing at the sight, Jason planted his feet on the floor and prepared to launch himself at the beast.

"Your friend was right. I do not wish to add murder to my list of sins, but if you do not leave here now, I will be forced to do so." Vincent tried to sound reasonable but only further enraged Jason.

"And leave Isabel behind? Never." Holding his hunting knife up, he gestured for him to come. "Let's see who is better?"

"Very well." The werewolf chuckled, the sound of it coming from his throat was grotesque to Jason's ears. "You wish to play the hunter? Then I will show you what it is like to be the prey."

The bones and muscles in Vincent's back began to crack and move. His snout grew longer and more pronounced as hair covered his face. The pants he wore ripped at the seams as his legs filled out, and his feet grew three times their size.

Jason had seen werewolves on television but they were make-believe. The real ones never showed their actual forms, not unless provoked and so no one really knew what they looked like. The world would have been a lot more terrified if they knew they would be up against an eight-foot giant.

Sucking in a breath, Jason didn't wait for Vincent to finish his transformation and charge at him. Knife at the ready, he ducked around the fur-covered beast and jumped on his back. He held on for dear life as Vincent bucked and clawed at him, trying to throw him off.

Jason tried to hold on with one hand and stab him with the other but he just couldn't get a steady grip. The monster was too big and too strong. If he had known what kind of being he was up against, he might have waited for back up, but one glance down at Isabel's form caused a renewed strength to course through him.

"You will never have her," Jason growled into the beast's ear. "Isabel is mine."

His hand reared back as he prepared to strike, but Vincent swiped out and caught him on the back, the sharp points of his claws piercing his skin. Jason lost his hold on him and fell to the ground where the werewolf turned on him.

Searing pain filled his back, and yet Jason's held his knife in front of him as Vincent approached. He couldn't die, not without saving Isabel first. He would fight this monster until his very last breath, and then he would fight some more.

Preparing to charge at the beast again, a gunshot sounded. Vincent's body tensed up, and he took a single step forward as if to attack before a white foam gurgled from his mouth, and he fell to the ground. Behind him, in nothing but her panties, stood Isabel holding Jason's shotgun.

A small laugh fell from his lips, a chuckle that turned into a groan at the wound on his back. Isabel rushed to his side. A choking sob came out of her, and he wrapped his arms around her even though it tore at his back.

"I was so scared, Jason," Isabel cried into his shirt, her hands clutching the fabric. "I didn't know what to do, I let him, he..." She hiccupped.

"Shhh. It's all right. I have you." He reassured her, stroking her hair. "It's over."

"But what about your back?" She jerked up, wiping her face, she tried to get him to let her see the damage. "Won't you get infected?"

"Would that bother you?" Jason cupped her face in his hands.

She shook her head and leaned her face against his. "I love you, Jason. I always have and always will, even if you go furry every once in a while."

"Guess that means we'll just have to do it doggy style then." Jason laughed when she smacked him on the arm and then drew her close when a voice called out from the hallway. "Oh, now they show up." He growled, before pulling his partially torn shirt over his head and shoving it onto her.

As they stood to greet the officers coming in, Luis groaned, lifting his head as he crawled from the floor. "What did I miss? Did you save her?"

Laughing at his friend, he gazed into Isabel's eyes. "No, she saved me."

# CHAPTER 16
## *ISABEL*

SITTING IN FRONT of her computer, Isabel groaned at the shortlist of prospective jobs available around Rollings. Three months after the incident with Vincent and she was still jobless. At first, she hadn't thought about getting a new job, too caught up in being with Jason and recovering from the whole ordeal with Vincent but now she couldn't put it off any longer.

"Any luck?"

Isabel looked up from the computer to Jason's hopeful face peeking into his office that she had taken over as her own. The last few months had been rough for both of them. Before the local authorities could keep it quiet, the news of Vincent's death had spread across the nation. No one in the area wanted to get involved with someone under the council's watchful eye.

"Not unless you want to move three hours away." She frowned at the screen.

Placing his hands on her shoulders, he worked on rubbing the tension from them. She dropped her hands from the computer and leaned back into his touch. The last few months had been more than enough work for her.

She and Jason had been called before the council on more than one occasion, being forced to recount the whole story to them about a dozen times. They couldn't seem to figure out how a tiny thing like her could take down a full-grown werewolf, and nothing could convince them that she wasn't covering for Jason.

Vincent's father came up from Minneapolis to collect his body and close up the casino, forgiving any debts owed to him. Even with that small blessing when they first met the stoic Alpha, Isabel had been afraid he would turn on them for killing his son. Fortunately, the werewolf had been more than sympathetic about Vincent's treatment of her and went so far as to apologize for his son's action. He had even called a counselor for Jason to help him through his first moon.

That night had been hard on everyone. Jason and his assigned counselor had set out at dawn and had hiked up into the forest. She had wanted to go with them, but his counselor had said it would be easier for him to focus on the change rather than keeping her safe. So, while they were off in the woods, Isabel had sat at home, not getting a wink of sleep. She had been too terrified of what the morning would bring.

She didn't have anything to worry about, though. The next morning Jason came home a bit dirty and roughed up but still him. He had been infected by Vincent and would have to have supervision for the next few months until they were sure he could keep his wolf under control.

People said she was crazy, to go from one werewolf to another, but she didn't mind. Jason had always been there for her, and she wasn't going to abandon him just because he was more of an animal than usual.

"You know, you could wait on getting a job for a while." His voice was cautious as if waiting for her to blow up at the suggestion.

"I've already waited long enough as it is. I can't keep mooching off of you." She glanced up at him. "I have to feel useful."

"You are useful. My books have never looked so good or my bed." He smirked at her, heat filling his eyes and making her ache.

"Not just that." She turned back to the computer, not able to help the small smile on her face.

"I mean, we could both take a break. Go somewhere." His hands dropped from her shoulders, and his presence moved away from her.

"Like where? What about your shop?" She twisted in her seat to look at him, only to find him on his knees before her with the box she knew had the ring she had thrown at him a year ago.

"I'm afraid I couldn't get the marching band on such short notice this time, and I know we really haven't talked about it, but I still feel the same way about you as the first time I proposed. So, I guess what I'm trying to say is," he paused, taking a deep breath. "Will you marry me?"

"Oh, Jason." She placed her hand on her heart, tears welling in her eyes.

"And we can wait on children if that is what you want," he quickly added before she could say anything one way or the other.

"Well, it's a little late for that." Then Isabel laughed at the confusion on his face. Deciding to put him out of his misery, she grabbed his hand and placed it on her stomach. "I'm pregnant, you brainless man."

Jason stared at her for a moment, the words still not making sense to him. Taking matters into her own hands, she took the ring out of the box and slipped it onto her finger. It was a little snug, the weight she had gained from all the exquisite food she had living with Vincent hadn't fallen off yet, and she suspected it was a lost cause now.

"You know," she continued as if he wasn't sitting in the middle of the floor like an idiot. "There is a new resort that just opened off the coast of Florida. In the Bermuda triangle of all places. They say the fae run it and it is impossible to get any kind of reception out there. Still, it's supposed to be really good for your health, and with the baby coming, I thought we could use all the boosts we could get."

"The baby?" The words fell from his lips as if he didn't understand their meaning.

"Yes, the baby." She shook her head at him, smacking him on the shoulder, a silly smile on her face.

"I'm going to be a father?" His words were quiet and unsure.

"Dear Lord." Isabel stood from her chair to stand before him. "Do I need to pee on a stick for you to get it through that thick head of yours? We are going to have a baby."

All of a sudden, she was off her feet and swinging in the air. Jason laughed and yelled out, "We're having a baby!"

"Yes," Isabel answered, her stomach rolling from all the spinning. "And unless you want the contents of my stomach coming out of me as well, you will put me down this minute."

Jason dropped her to her feet, still laughing, his face beaming with pride. "A resort, you said?" He started as if he hadn't missed the whole conversation. "What's it called?"

Getting her bearings, she pulled out the brochure she had tucked away from before and held it out to him. "The Never Isles."

Check out the BONUS side story featuring another fairy tale wolf!

# Red's One Night

# CHAPTER 1
## *ISAAC*

*STOP LOOKING AT her.* Isaac scowled at his clipboard, forcing his eyes off the woman who had been distracting him from his work since the moment she walked in the door of Albuquerque's Home for the Elderly.

*Come on, man, you're acting like you've never seen a pair of breasts before,* he scolded himself. Even if those breasts are the perfect handful and covered by a red sweater that hugged the curve of them just right.

Groaning, Isaac was happy there was a nurse's desk between him and the woman his cock was determined to stand at attention for.

"Are you okay?" Beverly asked a cute redheaded nurse who had been dropping hints that she was into him since he started working at the nursing home a few months ago. Isaac wasn't interested, though, she wasn't his type. Too small. Too breakable. Unlike red sweater.

"Fine," he grunted, "just hate paperwork."

"Don't we all," Beverly giggled and leaned in close to him, so her small chest pressed against his bicep. He couldn't help the way the muscle in his arm flexed at the brush of her breasts. He was a full-blooded male, what was he supposed to do?

"You know all this paperwork can be really stressful. Can get you wound so tight," she murmured low, giving him bedroom eyes. "We could maybe unwind together. Tonight, at my place?"

Isaac stroked his chin, the bristles of his beard scraping his fingertips. It has been a while since he'd been with anyone. He'd been too focused on getting out from underneath his father's thumb.

Isaac wasn't perfect. Not like his brother, Vincent. The perfect son. The perfect heir. The perfect werewolf.

Too bad their family had a history of anger management. He guessed that's where they differed. Vincent let his anger get out of control, Isaac wouldn't let that happen. That's why he went to anger management therapy every week and got a job that required him to have patience. He wouldn't be like his brother or his father who lashed out at the ones they loved.

Isaac gave the waiting redhead a cocky grin ready to accept her proposal but before he could, a full-throated laugh jerked his attention back to red sweater.

Sitting in a chair by her grandmother's bed, she threw her head back, her long dark hair cascading down her back as she laughed. Eyes closed, and her mouth open, flashes of her making a similar face as Isaac drilled into her came to the forefront of his mind. Just the image caused his raging cock tightened almost painfully.

"Uh, Isaac?" The sound of Beverly's voice pulled his attention from red sweater's face.

"Uh, not tonight," he muttered, turning his gaze back to the woman in the room across from the nurse's station. "Maybe another time?" he flashed Beverly a quick smile before rounding the desk.

"Where are you going?" Beverly asked, frowning hard. "Rounds aren't for another fifteen minutes."

Thumbing back to the room where red sweater was, he walked backward as he said, "Want to get a head start. Miss Jackson was giving me a hard time last time, better to be prepared."

"Oh, okay." She said her face a bit dejected, "let me know if you need any help."

"Don't worry, I got this." he shot her a cocky grin before heading into the room, intent on learning who red sweater really was and how he could get under it.

"MISS JACKSON, HOW are you feeling?" Isaac asked his eyes down on his clipboard, rereading the notes he had made when researching his patient. Miss Jackson had Alzheimer's. Her husband had died a year ago and has been going downhill ever since. Her only relatives included a daughter who has only been there once, and that was to put her in the home and a granddaughter who comes down every weekend or so from college.

"Oh, you know," Miss Jackson waved him off, huffing in her bed. "Everything aches, and my brain is full of noodles. I'm lucky to have this one here, or I'd be completely on the coo-coo train."

Red sweater placed her hand on her grandmother's, giving it a tight squeeze, "Oh, grandma. Everyone knows you're crazy, my being here doesn't change that."

Isaac was taken back by the granddaughter's words. He'd never speak that way to his elder, especially not one so ill as Miss Jackson. He was about to overstep his bounds and say something but Miss Jackson just laughed and wagged a finger at her granddaughter.

"It takes one to know one, Anna May." Miss Jackson's attention turned back to Isaac, her eyes scanning him up and down as if assessing his worth. "What do you think? Is my Anna just as crazy as I?"

Isaac gave Anna a once over, his eyes sliding up her long legs lingering at the apex of her thick thighs before they took in the red sweater that had been plaguing him all afternoon. A cough from Anna caused his eyes to jerk up to her face, where a delightful blush had flared across her cheeks. Once again, Isaac imagined what she'd look like while he had her at his sweet mercy. Would she blush like that? How far down did it go?

Letting his lips curl up into his signature panty-melting smirk, he replied, "Looks like a wild one to me."

If the sweet scent of her perfume hadn't been enough to drive him wild, the sudden flare of arousal that hit his nose almost staggered him. His dark eyes focused on her almost panting form, taking a deep breath in of her aroma. The beast inside of him paced back and forth, wanting nothing more than for him to take her right then and there.

"Well, I don't know about wild," Miss Jackson started, "but she sure is an odd one with her going for her Ph.D. in supernatural creatures. Can you believe it?" She laughed, shaking her head, "In my day, there was no such thing as supernatural let alone a whole study for it. If something strange happened, you pretended you didn't see it and get a stiff drink and move on with your life. Not my Anna here," she patted her granddaughter's hand with a genuine adoration.

"She's going to be the first ever supernatural doctor."

"Is that so?" Isaac cocked a brow at her, raising his hand to scratch the back of his head. The moment he did, Miss Jackson's eyes zeroed in on the bracelet on his wrist. A braided red and green cord that had a tiny wolf charm dangling from it.

Her delighted expression morphed into fear and hate as she pointed a shaky finger at him, snarling, "You. You get out of here, you mangy beast. I don't need the likes of you being around my granddaughter. She's a good girl. She is."

Isaac sighed and shook his head in defeat. "I'm not going to hurt your granddaughter, Miss Jackson. We've been over this before."

But it didn't matter what he said, she would hear nothing of it. She shrieked and hollered, throwing her cup and bedpan at him. Anna stood from her seat, trying to calm her grandmother but Isaac knew she had become inconsolable. The only thing that would calm her was for him to leave.

As was the story of his life.

# CHAPTER 2
## *ANNA*

IT WAS SO unlike her grandmother. She could be a bit kooky and inappropriate at times but she had never been hateful.

Anna didn't know what happened. One minute she was unskillfully trying to be sneaky in her efforts to get the hot nurse to ask her out, and then the next, she was freaking out. All because of the bracelet on his wrist.

She'd noticed a few people around wearing them but hadn't thought anything of it. For all, she knew it was a fashion statement or fundraiser for the locals. So she hadn't asked. But now she would.

Once she got her grandmother calmed and dozing off, Anna stepped out of the room and headed toward the nurse's station. When she stepped up to the station, she saw a cute redhead sitting behind the desk, her head down as she worked. After waiting a few moments for the nurse to notice her, she cleared her throat.

The redhead didn't glance up from her papers and snapped, "What do you need?"

Put off by her attitude at someone she had never met, Anna waited not saying anything until she finally looked up from her papers with a huff. The moment her eyes landed on her, the nurse's scowl deepened. "Can I help you?"

Frowning at the redhead's tone, Anna tapped the counter. "Where's the guy who was just in my grandmother's room?"

"Who? Isaac?" the redhead cocked a brow at her and then looked back at her forms, "He went on break. If you need anything, let one of us know."

He was on break? Had what her grandmother said bothered him that much he had to hideout? She hated to think that he had been hurt by her words.

Since the moment she had stepped into her grandmother's room, she had felt his eyes on her. Of course, she had. It was hard not to notice a drop-dead gorgeous guy like Isaac staring at her like he was wondering what she tasted like. But with looks like him, any girl would be stupid not to want him to find out.

He had dark hair that fell over his eyes but was cut short on the sides. A carefully trimmed beard that made her think of what it would feel like scrapping between her thighs as he took a taste of her. Just thinking about it now made her legs press together in need. No, a guy like him was hard to ignore and not one she wanted mad at her.

Anna turned from the counter and muttered, "No. I don't need anything." But then stopped and turned back to the redhead. "I changed my mind I do need something."

The nurse looked up from the desk, irritation flashing across her face, "Well, what is it?"

Ignoring her attitude, Anna gestured to her wrist, "Isaac, the male nurse, he was wearing a bracelet, a green and red one? My grandmother freaked out when she saw it. Do you know why?"

The redhead scoffed and turned back to her papers, "Because she's a prejudice old fuddy-duddy."

Anger billowed in her chest at the nurse's insult. "That's the thing. She's not. I've never seen her react that way to anyone. I mean, he didn't even look like a foreigner..."

"That's because he's not," the nurse cut her off. "Isaac's a werewolf. That's why he wears the bracelet. It lets medical personnel know that if his blood is spilled, it becomes a contaminated area, so no one else gets infected inadvertently."

A werewolf? Anna's brow furrowed. Of course, she was studying to work with supernatural but besides a Fae or two, she hadn't actually many. Especially, not a werewolf.

"Look," the redhead continued, with a condescending smile, "Don't feel bad. There are a lot of the older generations who aren't exactly open to change. Isaac, unfortunately, is used to it. But really, he's a good guy. Don't let his ailment cloud your judgment. Supernaturals are really just like you and me; some good and some bad.”

“Right,” Anna drew out and walked away from the desk and down the hall, her head full of jumbled up thoughts.

WALKING OUT OF the side door of the nursing home, Anna stopped short when she almost walked into the man himself. Or rather werewolf himself.

When he saw her, he dropped the cigarette he had been smoking, crushing it under his foot. He rubbed his hand across his mouth, a dark look in his eyes.

“Hey,” that one word, a kind of growl that rumbled out of his chest and straight to her core. How one word could affect her so much, Anna didn't know. All that mattered was she had found him.

“Hey,” she said back, inwardly smacking herself for being so lame.

They stood there for a few moments in awkward silence, more her than him. With her arms crossed over her chest, she tried to figure out what to say while sneaking glances at him from the corner of her eye.

Suddenly, a sexy chuckle came from him.

"What?" She turned to him, her question coming out more forceful than she meant it to be.

"You," he shook his head and laughed again. The sound of it caused a visceral reaction in her. "You are trying so hard not to look at me," he stretched his arms above his head, causing his shirt to pull up, revealing a thin expansion of skin that she had the sudden urge to lick.

"I'm assuming you found out what I am. So...?"

"So what?"

He spun around so fast she almost missed it. His face so close hers, she could smell the remanence of his cigarette. "Are you scared?"

Breath caught in her throat, her heart pounding in her ears, she gasped, "No."

"Really?" his hand reached up and tucked her hair behind her ear. The feel of his fingertips brushing her ear caused a shiver to run down her spine and into her toes.

"Yeah," she whispered and then cleared her throat, stepping back from him. "I mean, I wanted to apologize for my grandmother. I didn't know she felt that way about supernaturals. She had always been so supportive of my schooling. It surprised me."

Face turning severe, he crossed his arms over his expansive chest. "Don't worry about it. Knowing there are other beings in the world and actually meeting one is two completely different things. Believe me, some people are just stuck in their ways, even supernaturals."

"It still doesn't make it right," Anna shook her head and chewed on her lip. "Let me make it up to you."

His eyes lit up at her words, and he leaned into her a sexy smirk on his lips, "Oh really? And how are you going to do that?"

"A date," she spat out before she could stop herself, and then she quickly added, "I don't come to town often with school and all. And I don't really know the area, so I thought maybe you'd like to show it to me?"

His tongue snaked out to lick his lips and image of a wolf licking his chops came to her mind, the reaction to that thought wasn't a bad one. "I thought you were making it up to me? Showing you around sounds like I'm doing you a favor."

"So then I'll owe you twice." She held her breath, waiting for him to accept her proposal or laugh in her face at her pathetic attempt at getting a date.

He gave her that panty-melting grin of his and then said, "You've got a deal."

# CHAPTER 3
## *ISAAC*

JUST BEFORE SUNSET, he stood at a little wood outside of Albuquerque waiting for his important date to appear. He was surprised she had asked him out. It wasn't like he didn't get asked out all the time. Beverly had just done exactly that a few minutes before. But for the woman, he had been pining over for the last hour to just come out and ask him blew him away. It made him want to get to know her that much more.

When her grandmother had started freaking out on him, he would have thought she would be the same as her. She was too frightened of anyone different and not willing to change.

It was a stupid thought. Anna was a supernatural medical student. She would have to be more open-minded than that. She proved just that to him by asking him out rather than running the other way screaming.

They had agreed to meet about six p.m., and he started to wonder if it was all for show, and she really wouldn't show up at all. It had been a while since Isaac had been stood up, years in fact, and only because the girl had been sick and too embarrassed to call him and cancel.

The fact that Anna hadn't called to tell him she wasn't coming but was already thirty minutes late prickled at his nerves. She had wanted to meet him instead of him picking her up at her hotel room. Safety and all. He let her think that she was safe from him by meeting there but in reality, if he really wanted to find her, he could.

Her scent was ingrained in his mind. It wouldn't take much to find that spicy scent and follow it back to wherever she was staying. Even now, he could picture the look on her face when he showed up on her doorstep unannounced.

He imagined her mouth would fall open in surprise. A hint of fear would color her smell, making his blood rush with excitement. Then when she was over her initial shock, she'd welcome him in with open arms as well as open legs. He could almost taste her now, and then that taste turned into exhaust fumes, making him cover his nose in disgust.

His attention turned to the little road that led to the entrance of the woods, where a bright yellow taxi stood out against the trees. Arms crossed over his chest, he waited until the vehicle pulled up next to him. When it stopped, he opened the door to peer inside.

Still wearing that red sweater that made his mouth water, Anna smiled up at him from the back seat. She dug into her purse to pay the driver but Isaac handed the man a wad of bills before offering her his hand.

The moment their palms touched, it took all of Isaac's will not to throw her down on top of the taxi and ravish her. Her scent had spiked and the delicious smell of arousal filled his nostrils. If just the touch of his hand caused this much of a reaction in her, he couldn't wait to see how she reacted when he really put effort into it.

"Sorry I'm late," she looked up at him beneath long dark lashes, chewing on her lip in a way that made him want to kiss her. "I had a hard time getting a taxi, and then he didn't believe me when I said I wanted to come out to the woods. What are we doing out here exactly?" She scanned the area suspicion starting to fill her scent.

"You'll see." Grabbing her hand, he picked up the backpack he had sat on the ground while he waited and directed her toward the woods.

They walked a little way, the tension between the two so thick it would have choked a lesser wolf, but it only increased his need for her. Isaac waited to see how long it would take her before she started to ask questions once more. He was purposely being mysterious because he didn't want her to know much about the place. He didn't take women to where they were going. It was his place, his sanctuary.

He didn't have to wait long. They hadn't gotten more than a hundred feet into the woods before she tugged on his hand, stopping them in their tracks.

"Seriously, Isaac, if you don't tell me where we are going, I'm leaving." His name on her lips stern and irrefutable. He couldn't wait to hear her screaming it.

Isaac turned to face her, his hand holding the strap of his backpack. "I'm a werewolf where did you expect me to take you? Red Lobster? You can get that back at school but what you can't get," he stepped closer to her until she backed up against a tree, his arms caging her in, "is the whole supernatural experience."

Her eyes flickered to his lips and back up to his eyes a few times. He leaned in until his breath brushed against her mouth, and just as her eyes fluttered closed, her puckered lips expecting a kiss, he pulled away.

"Come on, it's just over her, not far now." Walking toward their destination, he looked over his shoulder to where she was still standing, confusion at what had just happened on her face. He resisted the urge to chuckle at the sight she made. Frazzled and by her scent a bit turned on, just the way he liked it.

He didn't wait for her to compose herself but kept walking, eventually hearing her footsteps following behind him. He pushed back a collection of brush to expose a rocky terrain filled with crumbling stone columns and buildings.

"Wow," the awe in her voice made his chest swell with pride. "This place is amazing. How did you find it?"

"I came across it while hunting one moon," Shrugging a shoulder, he helped her down into the heart of the area where there was a flat surface that used to be a wall of one of the buildings. "No one ever comes out here. It's the perfect place to let go and be myself."

"I suppose you don't get many chances of that in the city," she mused, her eyes on her surroundings but every once in awhile, coming back to peek at him.

Not answering, he set about taking the items he had brought for their date out of his backpack. He spread a blanket on the ground and patted it for her to have a seat. He pulled out a set of candlesticks and lit them, the sky already starting to darken around them, giving the area a romantic glow.

"You really thought all this out, didn't you?" She asked, sitting down next to him on the ground as he pulled more items from his bag.

He gave her a smug grin and handed her a Tupperware container, "I never do anything halfway. And I wanted this to be special for you."

"Why?"

Eyes intensely on her, he trailed his fingertips along the curve of her jaw, "You don't seem like the type who gives herself many breaks. From what your grandmother said, you work too hard. Who knows when you will let loose again?"

"I can let loose anytime I want to," she pouted her perfect lips at him, causing a tightening in his groin. He could just see them wrapped around his cock, his hand in her gorgeous hair as she drove him wild.

"Oh really?" he asked, his voice becoming low and husky.

"Yes, really," she leaned in toward him until their lips barely brushed. His wolf roared at him from the electricity that shot through them at that small touch.

Not one to deny his animal nature for too long, Isaac took the container from her and put it to the side. His chicken parmesan was good but not good enough to let this moment pass them by. His hands cupped her face, pressing his mouth to her. She reached up her hands tangling in his hair as she tugged on the roots, and each pull sent jolts of pleasure straight to his cock.

Isaac's tongue dipped out and coaxed her mouth open, the taste of her causing him to groan and lay her onto the ground. Shifting until his hips were between her thighs, he let her know exactly how she made him feel. The gasp that came from her mouth was enough to have him grinding his hardness into her core. He was about to take it a step further when she stopped him with a push of her hand.

"Wait, wait," she pulled in quick rapid breaths, "Just because I said I could let loose didn't mean I was going to have sex with you right here in the middle of the woods."

"Why not?" He smirked, his hand playing with the skin between that teasing red sweater and her jeans.

"Because," she frowned up at him though he could see it was a struggle for her to keep a straight face. "I'm not going to be another one of your conquests you got it on within your 'special place.'"

"You won't be another one because I've never brought anyone up here before."

She stared at him for a moment and then cocked a brow, "Really? Never?"

He laughed at the disbelief in her voice, "No, never. You'd be the first. You're the only one I thought would really appreciate it but if you would rather go back into town..."

He moved to get off of her when her hand curled into his shirt and jerked his body so that it was pressed against hers once more.

"Not in this lifetime."

THE HEAT OF the morning sun glared down on Isaac. He cracked open his eyes with a groan. His back was killing him. He made a mental note to remember not to sleep on the ground next time he came out there with a woman.

The mention of a woman caused Isaac's gaze to look to his left, where his date from the night before should have lain. Frowning at the empty space beside him, Isaac thought back to the night before.

After Anna had reinitiated their kissing, it had quickly escalated from a hot and heavy make-out session to clothes being thrown over the edge of the wall. Just thinking about how perfect her breasts had been in his hands and how responsive she had been to his touch made his morning wood even more prominent.

He couldn't remember the number of times she had let him take her. The first time had been a quick battle for dominance, one that he won, leaving her screeching into the night. The second time had been slower with her riding his cock as he watched her breasts bounce up and down in his face. His favorite time had been the last time. The one before they had both passed out from exhaustion.

They had been talking about their families while they caught their breath from their last session and she had brought up his father. As usual, when it came to his father, anger had billowed in his stomach, and he had used the only outlet he had to release it, her body.

He remembered the way he had slammed into her from behind, his hand wrapped in her dark hair. Each thrust caused her to cry out in a mix of pleasure and pain. She never asked him to stop or complained about how rough he was, and when he had reached his peak, he had howled out like the wolf he was.

Thinking back to it now, he felt a bit embarrassed. Was that why she had taken off without saying good-bye? Had he been too much of an animal for her to cope with?

Isaac wanted to say it wasn't possible, but it wouldn't be the first time a woman he'd slept with snuck out the next morning. Their excuses were always the same. He was too wild for them but what they really meant was they had gotten their supernatural itch scratched, and now they wanted nothing more to do with him. He wasn't 'bring home to daddy' material.

Scoffing, Isaac set about picking up the picnic they had never gotten around to eating the night before. Just as he started to fold up the blanket, he noticed a piece of paper that came fluttering out from underneath.

Brow furrowed, he almost didn't read it. It was probably like all the others, some thin excuse for leaving. But for whatever reason, his curiosity got the better of him. He picked the paper up and turned it over.

As he read it, the thin loopy handwriting made his face hurt with how hard he was smiling. Guess there were some decent women left in the world after all.

*Had an early flight to catch, didn't want to wake you. I had a great time. Hope to see you next time I come to visit grandma.*
*~ AM*

# About the Author

Erin Bedford is an otaku, recovering coffee addict, and Legend of Zelda fanatic. Her brain is so full of stories that need to be told that she must get them out or explode into a million screaming chibis. Obsessed with fairy tales and bad boys, she hasn't found a story she can't twist to match her deviant mind full of innuendos, snarky humor, and dream guys.

On the outside, she's a work from home mom and bookbinger. On the inside, she's a thirteen-year-old boy screaming to get out and tell you the pervy joke they found online. As an ex-computer programmer, she dreams of one day combining her love for writing and college credits to make the ultimate video game!

Until then, when she's not writing, Erin is devouring as many books as possible on her quest to have the biggest book gut of all time. She's written over thirty books, ranging from paranormal romance, urban fantasy, and even sci-fi romance.

**Want to be the first to know about Erin's new releases?**
www.erinbedford.com
Facebook.com/erinrbedford
twitter.com/erin_bedford
Erinbedford.com/newsletter